PERPLEXING EVIDENCE
From *THE ANATOMY OF MURDER* . . .

"Is there the slightest probability that without any temptation and with his pipe in his mouth—having only half an hour before been playing with his child, and just bought oysters for his wife and given them to the servant to prepare for supper—this unfortunate man should, no pistol having been seen in his possession about that time, go into the drawing-room in your presence, in the presence of your wife and his own, and commit a bungling attempt at suicide like that described by you? No person ever heard of such a thing in the annals of crime. . . ."

THE ANATOMY OF MURDER

Famous crimes critically considered by members of the Detection Club

HELEN SIMPSON
MARGARET COLE

JOHN RHODE
E. R. PUNSHON

BERKLEY BOOKS, NEW YORK

THE ANATOMY OF MURDER

A Berkley Book / published by arrangement with
The Detection Club

PRINTING HISTORY
First published in 1936 by John Lane/The Bodley Head
Berkley edition / November 1989

ISBN: 0-425-11834-7

A BERKLEY BOOK © TM 757,375
Berkley Books are published by The Berkley Publishing Group,
200 Madison Avenue, New York, New York 10016.
The name "BERKLEY" and the "B" logo
are trademarks belonging to Berkley Publishing Corporation.

PRINTED IN THE UNITED STATES OF AMERICA

10 9 8 7 6 5 4 3 2 1

Foreword

Four members of the Detection Club here offer commentaries upon an equal number of murders, some famous, others unknown to the general public. In each case the writer has not been content simply to retell the story of the crime, but has endeavoured to throw light upon it; either by revelation of new facts, or by application of psychological tests to the mind of the criminal, or by comparison of the resources of present-day investigation with those of the past.

Sir Thomas Browne provides the writers with a common viewpoint, and the book with its motto:

Tis not only the mischief of diseases, and the villany of poysons, that make an end of us; we vainly accuse the fury of Gunnes, and the new invention of death; it is in the power of every hand to destroy us, and we are beholding unto every one we meet, he doth not kill us.

31 Gerrard Street,
    London,
        August, 1936.

Contents

PART I

Death of Henry Kinder

by Helen Simpson

CRIME in Australia: those three words start, in the mind of the reader, a train of association which runs through the gold fields of Ballarat to end in the explosive sentiment of Rolf Boldrewood's *Robbery Under Arms*. Crime in Australia puts on a red shirt, gallops gallantly, tackles its trackers in the open air. The kindly spaces of a new country afford the criminal a chance, if he escapes, to make good; finally if he should have the bad luck to encounter Sherlock Holmes during his retirement, that finely tempered instrument of justice will say: "God help us! Why does Fate play such tricks with poor helpless worms?"[1] and refrain from prosecution.

So much for the popular conception. Actually, crime in Australia follows much the same patterns as crime elsewhere. Murders are committed for the same motives, gain, elimination, and fear; and the more sensational of these

[1]Conan Doyle: *The Boscombe Valley Mystery.*

1

are perpetrated by individuals whose surroundings would seem to guarantee their respectability.

Witness the case of that highly reputable chemist, John Tawell, of Hunter Street, Sydney, who having built a chapel for the Society of Friends, and publicly emptied six hundred gallons of rum into Sydney Harbour as an object lesson in temperance, in 1845 murdered his mistress with prussic acid and was hanged. Witness half a dozen other urban crimes, about which hangs no scent of the scrub or of saddle-leather; in particular, the murder of Henry Kinder, principal teller in the City Bank of Sydney, sufficiently well-to-do, living in a decent suburb on the North Shore of Sydney Harbour. This crime hath had elsewhere his setting; it is a domestic drama such as might have been played in any Acacia Avenue of the old world. True, the assassin had at one time some notion of dressing the part, and purchased a red Crimean shirt, on which bloodstains would not be conspicuous; but the crime itself was committed, so far as can be ascertained, in the ordinary sombre undress of a dentist.

II

On October 2, 1865, the news of Henry Kinder's suicide startled his circle of respectable friends. His tendency to drink was known, but that he should have had *le vin triste* to this degree was unsuspected; the more so that he had no troubles about money, and seemed to be happy in his family life. The inexplicable suicide became a topic of conversation in Sydney. Nobody had realized that Kinder was the kind of man to drink himself into delirium or to utter violent threats against himself and his family; yet that he had done so his wife declared at the inquest, and her evidence was corroborated. The coroner directed his jury to bring in a verdict of suicide during temporary insanity, and Kinder was buried with every testimony of regret and respect. Mrs. Kinder retired to Bathurst, where she took up life again with her parents, who kept a small general shop. The talk, for a time, died down.

But not for long. The jury found that the deceased had met his death "by the discharge of a pistol with his own hand." The How, thus was answered; the Why, despite evidence of his drinking, remained mysterious. It was this last question which worked in the minds of Henry Kinder's fellow-citizens, and there were conjectures in the clubs that a certain Louis Bertrand, who had been heard making extravagant statements concerning his relations with the Kinder family, might be able to answer it. These statements the police investigated, with the result that six weeks after the inquest, on November 29th, Louis Bertrand and his wife Jane were charged before the magistrates at the Water Police Court, Sydney, with the wilful murder of Henry Kinder; Helen Mary Kinder, the dead man's widow, appearing as accessory to the fact.

Bertrand was brought to court from gaol, where he had been serving a sentence for using threatening language. The warrant was read to him, it seems, in his cell. "Rather a heavy charge," was his comment. The detective inquired if he should take that by way of answer. "Am I on my trial now?" the accused asked sardonically; and being told that the officer was only stating the charge, Bertrand answered emphatically: "Then my reply to it is—not guilty." This he repeated in the dock. His wife echoed him. Mrs. Kinder, brought down in custody from Bathurst to Sydney, indignantly denied any knowledge of the crime. The magistrates heard these answers, refused bail, and at the request of the police remanded the prisoners until the Monday following, December 4th.

At that hearing nothing new was revealed, except the ages of the accused; Bertrand was 25 years old, his wife 21, and Mrs. Kinder, who refused to give the year of her birth, was stated to be apparently about 30 years of age. They were remanded again until December 7th.

III

On December 7th the case for the Crown was opened by Mr. Butler; and it at once became evident that Mrs. Kinder was on her trial, not as accessory to a murder, but as an adulteress. It was "morally impossible," said counsel, to commit the other prisoners without committing her also. The evidence would consist, in the main, of admissions made by the Bertrands, with other circumstances, all of which were capable of proof. The motive was easily discoverable. Certain writings, now in the hands of the police, would afford evidence that a personal intimacy existed between Bertrand and Mrs. Kinder; and, said counsel, with the ripe conviction of all Sydney's gossips behind him, "such an intimacy could not exist without furnishing a clue to the imputed crime."

Counsel proposed to establish that there had been illicit intercourse between Louis Bertrand and Helen Kinder before the death of the latter's husband; that it had been Bertrand's design to divorce his own wife; and that Henry Kinder had been killed in order that Mrs. Kinder might be free to marry Bertrand.

Detective Richard Elliott was his first witness. This officer produced a packet containing letters found in a drawer in Bertrand's house; they were unsigned, but appeared to be in the handwriting of Mrs. Kinder. He produced a diary found in an unlocked drawer in Bertrand's bedroom. He produced a bottle labelled tincture of belladonna, and a phial labelled chloride of zinc; together with a pistol and powder flask, a box containing caps, a tomahawk, a screw such as might be used for the nipple of a pistol, a phial of white powder, unlabelled, and two books. There was a brief interlude while prisoners' counsel elicited from the detectives concerned the fact that they had not been impeded or hindered in their search; Mrs. Kinder had even asked that a certain desk, to which she could not find the key, should be broken open. She told the officer that she kept none of Mr. Bertrand's letters, but always burned them after she had read them. He found one, however, dated October 28th, signed by Bertrand. He also found, in a box which contained children's clothing, a pistol; the pistol, Mrs. Kinder told him, with which her husband had shot himself. These cross-examinations over, Mr. Butler began to read from the letters of Helen Maria Kinder.

There were nine of them; and a more curious set of documents can seldom have been produced in evidence. There is not space to quote them fully. The picture they offer is of a woman alternately cautious and abandoned. News of her three children, of churchgoing, and of the life in a small country town make up the chief of their matter, but there are outbursts which leave no doubt as to her relationship with Bertrand. It is noticeable that these grow more frequent as she becomes more bored with the life of a small country town, unfriendly to a newcomer without money, inquisitive, uncharitable, and remote from the standards of a wider world. From first to last there is no mention of her husband, and no reference which would imply that she had any knowledge of how he came by his death.

The first letter, which begins: "My dear friend," and ends: "Kindest regards to yourself and all the family, and believe me ever to remain truly yours, Ellen Kinder," is by no means compromising. Fatigue—she had had two days' coach journey, looking after her three children the while—may possibly account for the non-committal tone of it. "I do not think I was ever so tired in my life; I trust I may never again experience such utter prostration." Bathurst appeared dreadfully dull, but she would not judge hastily. In the morning she intended going to church to have a look at "the natives"—not aborigines, but such society as the town offered. This is all, except that she sends her "kind love" to Jane, Bertrand's wife.

The next letter, written just a week later, is the queerest mixture of passion and practicality.

MY DEAREST DARLING LOVE,

I have just received your dear, kind, and most welcome letter. Oh, darling, if you could but know how my heart was aching for a word of love from you. Dear, dear lover, your kind loving words seemed to have filled a void in my heart. I cannot convey to you in words the intense comfort your letter is to me. It has infused new life into my veins. . . .

I suppose you must not be ashamed of our poor home when you come up, darling, but I know that will make no difference to you. If I lived in a shanty it would be all the same, would it not? Now about your coming up, dear darling. How I should like to see your dear face, and to have a long talk with you about affairs in general. But, my own love, I fear if you were to come just now you would not find it pay you. Everything is so dull, and what I fear more is that people to whom you owe money would be down on you directly, thinking you were going to run away. Dear darling, all this advice goes sadly against the dictates of my own heart, for my spirit is fairly dying for you. A glimpse of you, oh dearest, dearest, what would I not give to be taken to your heart if only for a moment; I think it would content me.

It is no use, dear. Your love is food—nourishment to me. I cannot do without it. I tried to advise you for the best, but I cannot. I cry out in very bitterness. If I could only be near you, only see you at a distance once again, I think I could bear myself. I believe, darling, if our separation is for long, I shall go out of my mind. . . .

How is Jane? What is the matter? It is of no use to say that I am grieved at her being laid up; that would be a mere farce between you and I. As to her assertions with regard to Mr. Jackson, I shall not answer them; for if I am to be taken to task about all she may choose to say about me I shall have enough to do. . . . I know her, and you ought to by this time. If you allow everything she may say to influence you against me, I have done, but, darling, I am yours. I leave my conduct to be judged by you as you think fit. There let the matter rest. It ought never to have been broached.

Mr. Jackson, at the time this letter was written, was serving a sentence of twelve months' imprisonment for attempting to extort money from Bertrand by threats. (He had written to Bertrand saying that his association with Kinder's wife was known, and could be proved if Jackson chose to say what he knew.) He was sentenced on the day—October 23rd—that Mrs. Kinder first wrote to Bertrand from Bathurst. He was to be an important witness at the trial, and Mrs. Kinder's airy ''It ought never to have been broached'' covers the consciousness that she had in fact lived with Jackson as his mistress. The document ends with an account of her family's money affairs. Her father's shop did not prosper, her mother had only £50 coming in yearly from some small property in New Zealand. They were not very easily able to keep four extra persons for an indefinite time. Could Bertrand discover some opening for the family in Sydney? An hotel perhaps? "I am always well when I get a letter to strengthen me." She ends: "God bless you. Good night, darling love, and plenty kisses from your own darling Child." In the third letter, dated November 9th, she is, as ever, preoccupied equally with the future and the present. She has tried for a governess's situation, but times are bad. The clergyman has come to call. Her youngest child, Nelly, would soon be walking. She would like to get into a dressmaking business in Sydney. The thought of seeing him again sends her blood "gurgling" in her veins. "God for ever bless you and preserve you from harm and preserve your dear children."

But Mrs. Kinder's mother was becoming suspicious, and, it would seem, not only of the relationship between her daughter and the Sydney dentist.

She advises me to be careful what we write, as she says there are many reports with regard to us in Sydney, and that the detectives have power, and might use it if they thought to find out anything by opening our letters. I was not aware they had that power; it is only in case of there being anything suspicious with regard to people.

Mamma, in fact, read her daughter a lecture, refusing to countenance "anything wrong". With all this, there was no question of turning away Mrs. Kinder and her children. "As far as anything in the shape of love and affectionate welcome goes, to the last crust they have I can depend." But the takings of the shop were never more than five shillings a day, and sometimes not sixpence. She could not go on being a burden; "I would rather be a common servant." Upon this situation she reflects:

How black everything looks, Lovey, does it not? Our good fortune seems to be deserting us.

Was this a reference to the death of Kinder, an affair surely of management rather than luck? If so, it is the only reference in the letters, which run to some ten thousand words. They keep their pattern of lamentations, shrewd planning, passion, and where her family is concerned a kind of affectionate independence, together with one or two items of actual news. She had become a seamstress to help the family finances; her father was off to New Zealand again; her brother Llewellyn was staying in Bertrand's house; she was determined to come to Sydney. The last letter, dated November 21st, ends:

When I think I shall be with you in less than a week— oh, this meeting, love, oh, I shall go mad; it is too delicious to dream of; oh, let it be in reality, darling, do, do. My feelings will burst, but still, dear one, I trust you will do what is best for us in the end, I would say——

The newspaper report says: "Remainder illegible."

IV

These were the first documents read by Mr. Butler, the Crown counsel. It is odd to picture the scene. The Water Police Court is not an impressive or a roomy building. The month was December, when Sydney is beginning to feel the weight of summer. There is great humidity, heat lies upon the town like a blanket, and all the distances dance. To Bertrand, even the stuffy court must have seemed spacious compared with his cell in Darlinghurst Gaol. Mrs. Kinder, brought down from the greater heats of Bathurst, may have found the air of Sydney grateful. Only Mrs. Bertrand, poor Jane, coming to the box from her pleasant house in Wynyard Square, must have felt bitterly the confinement and the heat. Mr. Butler, who had already spoken and read for some hours, returned to the charge in the afternoon; and when the diary's handwriting had been identified by Bertrand's assistant, Alfred Burne, he began, in the passionless tones congruous with his duty, to read aloud the diary of Louis Bertrand.

October 26th, Thursday.
Lonely! Lonely! Lonely! She is gone—I am alone. Oh, my God, did I ever dream or think of such agony? I am bound to appear calm, so much the worse. I do so hate mankind. I feel as if every kindly feeling had gone with her. Ellen, dearest Ellen, I thank, I dare to thank God, for the happiness of our last few moments. Surely he could not forsake us, and yet favour us as He has done. Tears stream from my eyes, they relieve the burning anguish of my bursting heart. Oh, how shall I outlive twelve long months! Child, I love thee passionately—aye, madly. I knew not how much until thou wert gone. And yet I am calm. 'Tis the dead silence which precedes the tempest. . . .

Do not rouse the demon that I know lies dormant in me. Beware how you trifle with my love. I am no base slave to be played with or cast off as a toy. I am terrible in my vengeance; terrible, because I call on the powers of hell to aid their master in his vengeance. God, what am I saying? Do not fear me, darling love. I would not harm thee, not thy dear self, but only sweep away as with a scimitar my enemies or those who step between my love and me. Think kindly of me—of my great failings. See what I have done for thee, for my, for our love.

Such were the first paragraphs of this document in madness. The diary was faithfully kept, reflecting Bertrand's love, his fantasies, his finances, and his health. In itself it would be enough, nowadays, to support a defence of insanity. But the magistrates of 1865 took it seriously, and Sydney shuddered as the newspapers reported it piecemeal. The journal covers only twenty-four days, from the date on which he parted from Mrs. Kinder to that on which he was summoned on the charge of writing a threatening letter to a woman, Mrs. Robertson. His triumph over Jackson makes odd reading, when it is considered that three weeks later both were serving sentences for a parallel offence.

In the train I borrowed half the *Empire*, which contained this paragraph: "Francis Arthur Jackson, convicted of sending a threatening letter to Henry L. Bertrand with the intent to extort money, sentenced to 12 months' hard labour in Parramatta Gaol." It pleased me. I am satisfied. Thus *once more* perish my enemies. He is disposed of for the present.

On the same page:

I feel that I love you as mother, sister, husband, brother, all combined. What work I have before me, God only knows, but I will call His love to help me, and strive to do right. I feel I shall. Thy dear devoted love will save me. I know it will, and we may yet be good and happy together.

An echo of the gossip which was alive concerning him may be found in the brief statement which follows: "Am doing no business whatever." He was ill, too, with some internal trouble, concerning which he makes this reflection:

I am now, by my own agonies, paying a debt to retributive justice; how and what I have made others suffer, God only knows; but I have, I richly deserve all I now feel; and you, my love, *have you not done the same*?

'Tis strange our two natures are so much alike. I love a companion who can understand my sentiments, respond to the very beating of my heart, help me to think, to plan, and by clear judgment advise me on worldly affairs. A woman is not a toy. Women are as men make them. I have found, from experience, that half the trouble women give their husbands is caused by the husbands themselves—sometimes directly, but often from some indirect cause that might have been avoided if the man had used even moderate care in the guidance of the being sacredly entrusted to his charge. . . . One more day stolen from fate.

This was Friday, October 27th. Two days later he was up and about, spending an artistic rather than a conventional Sunday.

I awoke this morning too late for church—I did not dress or shave. I fear, my dear Nelly, that not having

you to fascinate I shall become slovenly and untidy, for
if I consulted my own feelings I should not dress at all.

I want fame, as well as wealth and power, and as
usual little Bertrand must have his way. You know he is
a spoilt child, spoilt in more ways than one. So as I was
saying, I must have fame, fortune and power, as well
as the most ardent, pure, passionate, and devoted love
of the most fascinating, amiable and best of women that
the world at present contains. There, if this is not flat-
tery I do not know what is; but it is the truth—at least,
I think it is the truth to the best of my belief, as we say
in court. Oh, I must not speak of courts; we have had
enough of them, at least for the present.

At this time he set to work to model two salt-cellars for
the third Victorian exhibition of 1866; Fijians, "kneeling
in a graceful attitude", holding pearl shells, upon stands
"emblematical of the sea shore"; the spoons to consist of
paddles, "formed of some sort of shell, small of course";
all to be cast in solid silver, frosted. "Dearest, it is for
thee that I toil." He turned from this work to conversations with his sister, who recommended a divorce as being
the kindest thing that he could do for poor Jane; and to
his diary, intended for Ellen's reading later on, when the
period of separation was over. Certain further passages of
this were read with emphasis by Mr. Butler.

I should feel ashamed of my love, of what I have done
for it, if it were no different from that of others. That is
our only excuse, whether on earth or Heaven, for what we
have accomplished. . . . Let us not be cowed or terrified
at aught that besets us. I warned you what to expect, and,
dearest, for the greatness of our love for one another,
surely we can bear fifty times more than we have to bear.

I do not fear the result. To me the end is clear and palpable, I am sure of it; I never yet failed in my life.

November 8th.

Thank God, another day gone. However will a twelve month pass? God only knows. My heart grows sick and faint when I look into the future. Oh, God, is this Thy retribution for our sins? Did I flatter myself that the Almighty would let me—a wretch like me—go unpunished; but I tell thee, fate, I defy thee. I feel as though my heart were rent in pieces, and then dark thoughts obtrude themselves before me, fiends rise and mock me; they point to a gate, a portal through which I feel half inclined to go; but not yet. What would my love do without me? . . . No matter what thou hast been, my child, I hold thee as a true, virtuous wife to me, for you have been true to me, my dearest love.

Bertrand went on this day, Wednesday, to see one of the directors of the City Bank, Kinder's employers, who gave him news. A temporary cross was to be put on "poor Harry's grave" in New Zealand (whence the Kinders had come to New South Wales); "they think that Harry did not intend to kill himself, but only to frighten his wife." When Bertrand suggested that possibly Mrs. Kinder might come to Sydney to find work, the director was evasive and recommended that "old affairs should blow over". Next day Mrs. Kinder's father, Mr. Wood, came to see him, and they walked down together to the ferry wharf, and travelled over to the North Shore to see a mutual friend, De Fries.

I felt very strange. This is the first time I have been to the Shore since poor Harry's funeral. I am standing

on the deck, my face turned towards the little house
with the two chimneys, as I used to do when on wings
of love I flew to my beloved. . . . How horribly jealous
I was, I was mad . . . surely there can be no worse hell
than our own conscience.

Mr. De Fries it was who gave Bertrand the first warning
that all was not well, and that Sydney, unlike New Zealand, was beginning to be suspicious of Kinder's suicide.
De Fries spoke reasonably; said that he had watched the
affair growing; and that he had a high regard for Jane. He
told Bertrand that Mrs. Kinder cared nothing for him, that
she was a calculating woman, while Jane was an affectionate and true one. He felt for Bertrand, he told him, like a
brother, and exhorted him, if he cared for his happiness
in this world and his welfare in the next, not to yield to
temptation. The diarist listened attentively, but coming
home, broke Jane's fan in a passion. That he believed, or
rather, that he knew De Fries to be speaking the truth, is
shown in a paragraph which ends the entry for this day:

November 12th.
Be she as wicked as Satan, as vile and wily as the
serpent, I, even I, will save her, will raise her from the
depth of hell. I, Ellen, even I, thy lover, wicked as I
am, will be a Saviour to thee. Dear, sweet, loved Ellen,
the more they oppose us the greater will be my power
of resistance. Poor fools, to try and thwart my will.
Indeed, if thou hast me for an enemy—I who value human life as I value weapons, to be used when required
and thrown away or destroyed; some, of course, kept
for future use if necessary. Beware! If I have my way
in this, if I obtain this sole object of my being I feel
that I shall be reclaimed; but if not, no matter from

what cause, Heaven help the world, oh! I shall indeed
be revenged.

Next, Mrs. Robertson, a friend to both parties, issued
her warning. She advised Bertrand to have no more to do
with Mrs. Kinder; and told him frankly that she would not
have Ellen in her house, were she to come to Sydney.
Again he listened patiently, and again there followed an
outburst, a frantic act of faith.

DEAR, DEAR CHILD,
    I trust that she is truly penitent for what she has done,
and that with me she will be in future a truly good and
virtuous woman. Why do people try to torture me thus?
God knows I have misery and wretchedness enough. I
am prepared for the worst and God help the world if
this my forlorn hope fails. To hear her [Ellen] spoken
of as bad, is sufficient to upset my intellect. . . .
    Ellen, my dear love, I must be near you. I want to
look into those dear wicked eyes and I know they cannot, will not, deceive me. If I have, like others, cause
to repent what I have done—I must drop this painful
subject or I shall be ill—it will unman me—unfit me for
the battle I am fighting. Enough excitement of mind for
one day. Adieu, my thoughts. Adieu, my own Ellen.
                                                    Louis.

It is not quite the last entry, but it is the most revealing
of all. The exaltation was fading; the way to happiness,
which had seemed so clear and sure, was obscured. Bertrand knew that Mrs. Kinder had been the mistress of at
least one of his acquaintances; that there had been other
men in New Zealand he conjectured. He was tormented;
the journal plainly shows him twisting away from inescap-

able conclusions, and so towards madness. When Mr. Butler laid down the notebook which gave such an intimate picture of Bertrand's mind, he had proved to the public's satisfaction that Bertrand had good reason to wish Kinder out of his way.

V

But Kinder met his death by the firing of a pistol close to his ear. Whose finger pulled the trigger of that pistol? Mr. Butler recalled Bertrand's assistant, Alfred Burne, who, after telling how he delivered letters from Bertrand to Mrs. Kinder, and how she had often stayed in the surgery at night, gave the following account of some remarkable expeditions:

> About six weeks previous to Kinder's death he [Bertrand] asked me where I could get a boat to hire. I mentioned Buckley's among others. We went rowing the following night about 12 o'clock, to the North Shore as far as Kinder's house, opposite to the bedroom window on which the moon was shining. He said: That is his bedroom. He did not then say what was the purpose of his visit. He did not go in. He said the moon was too strong, he had come too early. . . . We went back again three nights after, taking a boat from the same place, and went up to the house. As we went over he said it was very likely that next morning Kinder would be found dead in his bed, having committed suicide, and that letters from Jackson would be found in his hand.

They arrived at Kinder's house about one in the morning. Bertrand took off his boots, gave them to Burne to hold, and climbed into the house by the dining-room win-

dow. He came back much later—Burne fell asleep meanwhile—angry because Kinder would not drink his beer,
and consequently was awake. "We had drugged it," said
Bertrand.

Some days, about a week later, Bertrand produced in
his surgery a hatchet, and asked Burne to bore a hole in
the handle so that he might tie it under his coat by a string.
A young man, Ranclaud, who was staying in the house,
asked what he meant to do with it. Bertrand answered
abruptly, and with no care for probabilities, that he was
going fishing, and went out with Burne to their hired boat.
On the way, he said that Kinder had insulted him; that he
was going to knock Kinder's brains out first, and then get
a divorce from Mrs. Bertrand.

I remarked what object could he have in putting Mr.
Kinder out of the way when Mrs. Kinder was as good
as a wife to him. He said he wished to have Mrs. Kinder
all to himself.

On this occasion Bertrand entered the house by the same
window, but returned soon, saying that Jackson and Mrs.
Kinder's brother Llewellyn were sleeping in the house,
and as the boards creaked he did not think it safe.

COUNSEL: Safe to do what?
BURNE: To murder Mr. Kinder, as I understood.

A week later the expedition was repeated, but in remarkable conditions. Bertrand shaved himself at midnight;
then blacked his face, donned a mask and the red Crimean
shirt, topped this disguise with a slouch hat, took off his
boots, drank some brandy, and set out in the boat at about
1.30 in the morning. Burne went with him. Why he should

have done so is inexplicable. True, he was in Bertrand's employ; true, he may not have taken seriously Bertrand's boasts and threats against Kinder. But he was sufficiently well aware of danger when his own skin was in question.

On these occasions I always carried the hatchet myself; I also used to get him to sit in front of me in the boat for fear of accidents. I made him pull the stroke oar, while I pulled the bow oar, fearing that, taking me by surprise while my back was turned, he might throw me into the water.

That night Bertrand asked Burne to help him when he got inside the house. If Kinder, he said, were to be killed that night, suspicion would inevitably fall on Jackson, who was leaving Sydney next day. The young man answered that it was all too romantic for him, that he had no share in Mrs. Kinder and intended to run no risk. Bertrand at this seemed to abandon his plan, whatever it may have been, and they rowed home. This was the last expedition in the boat.

But not the end of Bertrand's fantastic preparations. His next act was to cut off his moustache, dress as a woman, and go with Burne to buy two pistols at a pawnshop in Lower George Street, then a fairly tough locality. On the day following this purchase he acquired a sheep's head, and began to practise shooting at it in his surgery with bullets he had made himself in a mould. His wife and her mother ran in at the first shot, alarmed, naturally enough, by the noise and smell of smoke. This was on a Saturday. On Monday morning Burne was told to destroy the broken skull in the furnace, and did so. That afternoon he heard that Kinder was dying.

At this point we get Bertrand's own version of the tragedy as he told it to Burne on his return from Kinder's house. Kinder, he said, had actually shot himself as the result of a practical joke. The two men had left the house and their wives in search of a pub and a drink. On their way back Bertrand had suggested that the women should be given a fright, and produced a pistol, which he said had no bullet in it, but only powder and a wad. Kinder, who was drunk, agreed to put it against his head and fire; and when they came to the room where the women were, actually did so, with the result that the charge of powder drove the wad into his ear and jaw. Proof of this, said Bertrand, was that no bullet could be found.

It was a fantastic story, but Bertrand's counsel seized upon it, and later there was great argument about it and about when the doctors came upon the scene. Unfortunately, Bertrand, forgetting this sketch of a possible defence, later admitted to Burne that his wife had found a bullet, and produced from his pocket a flattened scrap of lead which he said was the bullet in question. Burne secreted one of those that had been made in the surgery to fire at the sheep's head, and gave it to the detectives; this bullet fitted the second of the pawnshop pistols.

Defence counsel could not do a great deal with Burne. They could prove him a poltroon, but by no means could they prove him a liar. The butcher who had sold the sheep's head, the pawn-broker who had sold the pistols, Buckley the boatman, Mrs. Bertrand's mother who had witnessed the pistol practice—all these in turn corroborated his story. Asked why he did not attend the inquest and there tell what he knew, he answered that he had not been subpœnaed. Asked why he had gone to the detective office afterwards with information, he gave the following answer:

It was slightly for the sake of public justice, and by way of protecting my life that I went there, the object being self-preservation in particular, the other in a slight degree.

This naïve statement virtually ended his evidence. His last admission was to the effect that he, Burne, had read part of Bertrand's diary before the detectives came; then he was told to stand down, having proved himself a useful though contemptible witness for the Crown.

VI

After certain corroborating witnesses came one Alexander Bellhouse, employed in the Government Service, who had known Bertrand for some years. He repeated an extraordinary statement made to him by Bertrand a month before the trial. After a game of cards at the house in Wynyard Square, Bertrand had accompanied him to the door as he was leaving, and told him that he was responsible for the death of Kinder. "He said that he was sorry for Kinder but wanted him out of his way." He also told Bellhouse that he was a powerful mesmerist, and could do anything he liked with people. His wife knew of his attachment to Mrs. Kinder. He stated that he had put the pistol in Kinder's way, not that he had shot him. The witness was so greatly shocked by Bertrand's statement and manner that he "could not sleep that night because of it". The impression left on his mind was that Bertrand had somehow compelled Kinder to shoot himself.

Harriet Kerr, Bertrand's sister, followed Bellhouse with an even more remarkable story.

Early in the morning Bertrand came into my bedroom as I was washing the baby. He said, "Stay a

minute, I have something to say to you." He told me
to sit on the side of the bed and asked if I had read
of the death of Kinder. I said I had. He paused a
little, then said, "Kinder did not shoot himself. I shot
him." I replied, "You must be mad to say such a
thing!" He said, "No, I am not mad. I tell you I did
shoot him." I said, "But how cruel of you to do so,"
and put my hands up to my face. He pulled them
down again. I was crying, and he said, "Don't cry. I
don't regret what I have done." He said when he had
shot Kinder he put the pistol in his hand and a pipe
in his mouth.

Three weeks later Mrs. Kerr had another talk with her
brother. This time his wife was present, but asleep. "She
used," said Mrs. Kerr, "to sleep a great deal. It was more
like stupor." Bertrand said that he did not want to have
to kill Jane, and that a divorce would be better, if he could
get up "an adultery case with a respectable married
woman". His sister took him to task bravely about his
behaviour in general and this plan in particular. Jane had
done him no harm, she told him, and Mrs. Kinder was a
wicked woman. He knew that, he said. She was wicked
already, and he would make of her a second Lucrezia Bor-
gia. It was very likely, he intimated, that before his sister
went to Brisbane she would find herself attending his wife's
funeral. Mrs. Kerr went on to describe an attempt upon
Jane's life. At one o'clock in the morning there was an
argument, and Bertrand, taking up a life-preserver, threat-
ened his wife, who cried out in terror the strange words:
"Don't kill me. You promised on your word of honour
you would not kill me." Mrs. Kerr went to the top of the
kitchen stairs and called the servant, then went up again
to the first landing, having heard the parlour door open.

Her brother was saying: ''Now Jane, I want you to go into the surgery. I want you to write on this piece of paper that you are tired of your life.'' She refused, saying that he might pour poison down her throat, but she would write nothing. He seemed to abandon his intention, gave her a glass of brandy and water, and sent her to bed in Mrs. Kerr's room. Poor Jane sat down upon a chair, and there and then, to her sister-in-law's astonishment, fell fast asleep.

Now comes an account of the death of Kinder. It is necessarily second-hand; the three persons who took part in the scene were in the dock, and so unable to give direct evidence. But Mrs. Kerr's recollection of what she had been told was very exact, and there is no reason to suppose that Mrs. Bertrand's story was fabricated.

On the morning of the first Monday in October Mrs. Bertrand was told by her husband to take the baby and accompany him to the Kinders' house on the North Shore. It was a rainy morning, and she was reluctant that the baby should go out; however, as always, she yielded. When they arrived at the house Bertrand seemed more serious than usual, and more gentle with Mr. Kinder. He walked up and down the room very fast, gloved, and with one hand in his pocket. Jane and Mrs. Kinder were looking out of the window when they heard the report of a pistol. They turned, to see a pistol dropping from Kinder's hand as he sat in his chair, and Bertrand taking a pipe from the table which he stuck in Kinder's mouth. Mrs. Kinder ran from the room in terror; Bertrand followed, and forced her to return. He then took his wife's arm in a terrible grip, and made her face the shot man, from whose head blood was flowing. ''Look at him well,'' said Bertrand, ''I wish you to see him always before you.''

Jane bathed the wound, while Mrs. Kinder and Bertrand

walked up and down the verandah embracing. She found a bullet, flattened, which had dropped against the wainscot, and showed it to her husband when he next entered the room. Bertrand took it from her, saying it was just what he wanted, and she never saw it again.

But Kinder did not die of the wound in his head. A doctor was called, with whose help Jane got him to bed; she then took up her abode in the house and nursed him faithfully for four days, at the end of which time he appeared to be recovering. When she told her husband so, Bertrand in rage said that he must not live; poison should end him if a bullet could not. He made Jane "mix the poison"; and Mrs. Kinder gave it in milk to Kinder, who died soon afterwards.

This was Jane Bertrand's story of the crime. It was told to and recounted by her sister-in-law, Harriet, to whose presence in the house in Wynyard Square Jane may have owed her life.

I wished to protect Mrs. Bertrand, in fact that was what I stayed in the house for, and I must also add, I stayed partly in fear of my life. We were always in dread of our lives. He [Bertrand] did not appear to wish me out of the house, but quite the contrary. . . . I was his favourite sister, though he did not show it by his manner. He was often very eccentric. Even in gaping he would imitate the roar of a tiger and had done it in the street. . . . Bertrand often told me, at that time, that he had a great mind to murder Mrs. Bertrand and say I had done it.

VII

This evidence concerning poison was something quite unexpected by the public. The verdict at the inquest had been death by shooting, and the possibility that Kinder might have died from any other cause had not been considered. The Crown witnesses were elusive on this point. A chemist who had analysed the contents of the stomach found no traces of poison, but stated that, since certain vegetable poisons rapidly decomposed in the stomach, this analysis did not rule out the possibility that they had been employed. He was asked if aconite or belladonna came within this category of untraceable substances. (Aconite and belladonna were found in Bertrand's surgery.) He replied that they did; that one or the other might have been administered, as was asserted, on October 6th; but that now, two months later, it was a matter impossible to be proved.

The Crown accordingly let this point go, and called up the surgeons who had performed the post-mortem. They agreed as to the nature and direction of the wound. The shot had blown off the ear and broken the lower jaw; the brain itself was not touched. In short, of such a wound a man in good health and of temperate habits need not have died. But Kinder was not in good health, and he had been drinking heavily for months. He had lost a good deal of blood, and to this haemorrhage, with the shock and subsequent exhaustion, all three doctors attributed his death.

On one matter they disagreed, and here was a point eagerly caught at by the defence, since it seemed to square with what Bertrand had told Burne on the evening of the murder. Bertrand's story then was, that the whole affair was an accident, and that the pistol had been charged with powder and a wad only. No bullet had, in fact, been found in the skull by the doctors who conducted the post-mortem examination. Was it possible, asked Mr. Robberds, for the defence, that Kinder might have done as was suggested, pulled the trigger of a pistol charged but not loaded, and that the wound, which extended from the top of the ear to the lower angle of the jaw, could have been caused by gunpowder and wadding only?

Dr. Alloway, who had served in the Crimea, and had seen many gunshot wounds during his service in India as an army surgeon, gave it as his opinion that such a thing was not possible. He maintained that the external condyle of the lower jaw showed marks of having been struck by some hard substance at the point of fracture; and that wadding from a pistol could never have broken so thick a bone, no matter how great the charge of powder behind it.

Dr. Allayne did not see "anything to indicate that the injury was caused by a round substance such as a bullet". The force of the explosion alone, he declared, was sufficient to cause such a wound—that is, if the pistol were held close to the head.

Dr. Eichler came to the conclusion that the wound had been self-inflicted, but would not give an opinion as to whether or no it was a bullet that had caused the damage to the jawbone.

If the description of the direction of the wound is correct, it is difficult to see how it could have been self-inflicted. The bullet, or wad, whichever caused the damage, had entered behind the right ear, detaching the ear itself from the scalp, and continued its course forward and downward to break the jawbone on the right side. It is quite extraordinarily difficult for a man to hold a pistol so as to inflict such a wound upon himself; the trigger must be pulled with the thumb, and the head must be turned down and to the left at a painful angle. On the other hand, if the shot

were fired by a right-handed man standing behind a seated
man, the direction of the wound is easily accounted for.
(According to Jane Bertrand's story, Kinder was seated,
and Bertrand standing or strolling, at the time when she
heard the shot fired.) There is the possibility that a suicide
might point the barrel of his weapon at his jaw; but the
doctors were agreed, from the evidences of powder black-
ening, that the missile, whatever it may have been, entered
behind the ear.

It might be supposed that the case for the Crown was
by this time strong enough; but there were two more witnesses to come. Francis Arthur Jackson was brought to
Sydney from Parramatta Gaol to give evidence concerning
the triangular relationship between Kinder, his wife, and
Bertrand. Agnes Mary Robertson, whose charge of using
threatening language had brought Bertrand to Darlinghurst, appeared to testify to the dentist's frantic and unreasonable rages.

VIII

Jackson had an unsavoury story to tell. He had known the
Kinders in New Zealand, where he had been intimate with
the woman; this intimacy was resumed when, six months
before the date of Kinder's death, he came to live in their
house on the North Shore. Bertrand was a frequent and
difficult visitor, who showed his feeling for Ellen Kinder
very plainly, and made it clear to Jackson that he would
not tolerate a rival.

> During a conversation with Mrs. Kinder, as she saw
> Bertrand coming in she said I had better go. I said no,
> I thought not. I asked her when Bertrand was there
> which of the two men she preferred. Bertrand would

not speak to me at first. . . . He asked Mrs. Kinder if she cared for him, and she bowed her head. He said he wished to remove any thought from my mind that Mrs. Kinder had cared for me from the moment she saw him.

On another occasion while I was lying in bed and he was standing at the foot of it he reiterated how very fond he was of Mrs. Kinder, that he would do anything for her, and I must not be surprised at anything I might hear after I went away. He had given me some money to go away, and said: "You would not like to be implicated in a charge for the murder of Kinder?" I said: "No, I should think it impossible." He said if I stayed in Sydney I might be implicated. I said it was impossible, and he said there were many stranger things in the country than that. He said in a year or two he would marry Mrs. Kinder. I said it was impossible, her husband being alive. He said: "All things are possible, and time will show."

Bertrand offered to pay my passage to Melbourne, and held the threat over me that if I did not go I might be implicated in Kinder's death, and remarked about the Devil having a strong will.

Jackson went to West Maitland, apparently moved by this threat. It is odd to see with what assurance Bertrand shifted about the pieces in his lunatic game, and difficult to account for their docility. Jane's submissiveness came from terror, or possibly from the administration of drugs; her stupors and dozings, which were observed not only by her sister-in-law but by visitors to the house, seem to lend colour to this explanation. She was wholly in Bertrand's power, and so maintained by his occasional and mysterious threats against the children. Not so Burne, an employee, who could leave his service when he chose; a young man with his wits about him, and over whose head Bertrand held no threat, so far as the evidence goes. And not so Jackson, another free agent.

Yet Burne did errands which he must have known were dangerous, and escorted his employer on expeditions whose confessed object was murder. Jackson, who was in a strong position to defy him, established as he was in the Kinders' house, and the lover of Mrs. Kinder; Jackson who had only to report these threats to the police to be rid of his rival; Jackson took himself out of the way obediently, and for a time held his tongue. True, he wrote a blackmailing letter later, when he learned of the coroner's verdict on Kinder; but he was not a subtle man, and there is no reason to suppose that he took himself off in order to leave Bertrand free to commit a murder from which he thus might draw some profit. Nor was it a fact that he was tired of Mrs. Kinder. He was still intent upon her, and took such steps as he might to see her alone.

After my intimacy with Mrs. Kinder commenced I had an object in getting him [Kinder] to drink to excess That was, to get him stupid so as to afford me opportunities for interviews or intimacy with Mrs. Kinder. The human mind is very base. I was base enough for that. By constant drinking with him I thought it would shorten his days. It would shorten anybody's days.

That Mrs. Kinder had anything to do with the murder he refused to believe. She had constantly tried to prevent Kinder from drinking in New Zealand and after they came to Sydney. She was not present at any of the conversations when Bertrand hinted that Kinder might die. She had tried to do her duty as a wife.

I remember her saying that she would rather not have anything to do with either of us, that she intended to do her duty as a wife. At that time she requested me to leave her, and never to come near her again. Any interviews I had with her were of my own seeking. She told me she feared Bertrand. She said: "He seems to be a perfect devil," and spoke of him as being able to make her do things against her will, having a sort of clairvoyance [sic] over her, or mesmeric influence. There is nothing that I know of to incriminate her in this charge beyond intimacy with Bertrand.

He did the best he could for the accused woman, but the fact of the confessed relationship between her and Bertrand deprived his testimony of weight. A jury was not likely to be much impressed by his picture of practical Ellen Kinder as the helpless victim of a mesmerist, even though this theory found corroboration in the recollections of the witness who followed him.

So much for Jackson. Mrs. Robertson, on whose account Bertrand was undergoing imprisonment, spoke of Bertrand's mesmeric influence, which she had felt upon more than one occasion.

When I felt a dizziness in my eyes I ran out of the room. I know he has tried to mesmerize me by following me about the house, and looking at me. He compelled me that night to kiss him in the presence of Mrs. Kinder, and made me feel very unwell. Since then I have kissed him to save his wife from violence. He said: "Do you intend to do as I bid you?" I said no. He then called his wife so that he might flog her unless I kissed him, and to save her from violence I did so.

Mrs. Robertson too had been obliged to listen to threats against Kinder, and to confidences concerning the murder. Bertrand had been at her house on Thursday, the night before Kinder died; he fell on the floor there in a kind of fit, calling: "Bring the milk and mix the poison." He declared that he must go next day and confess that it was he who fired the shot. He told a fantastic story of having bought pistols at Kinder's request, that he might fight a duel with Jackson. He maintained that it was Mrs. Kinder's suggestion that her husband should be shot while Jackson was in the house, in order that the blame might fall on him.

A chemist was recalled, there was a question or two concerning the poisons generally used in the practice of dentistry, and the case for the Crown, at this first hearing before the magistrates, closed. The magistrates refused to dismiss Mrs. Bertrand, refused bail all round, and committed all three prisoners for trial at the next sitting of the Criminal Court, to be held on Monday, December 18th.

IX

Before the prisoners came to trial, Jane Bertrand was set free. There was no evidence that she knew anything of Bertrand's preparations, and although she was, by her own confession, in the room at the time when the murder was committed, nobody could suppose that she had had any hand in it. Motive lacked wholly. She was aware of the relationship between her husband and Kinder's wife; it was not to be credited that she should connive at a crime whose sole object was to bring them together, or that she should not do all in her power to hinder a death by which, as she might have suspected, her own was foreshadowed.

Nor could a sufficient case be made out against Mrs.

Kinder. Her letters, though they showed her to be infatuated with Bertrand, nowhere gave any least hint that she shared his guilt as a murderer. Bertrand's accusations against her, made to Mrs. Robertson, were unsupported; and though she showed some callousness (if Jane's account is to be believed), walking up and down with Bertrand's arm round her waist while her husband lay bleeding, and also, according to Mrs. Robertson, driving with Bertrand in a 'patent safety' hansom on the Friday that he died, there was no actual proof of her complicity. Jackson's statement—'' there is nothing that I know of to incriminate her in this charge beyond intimacy with Bertrand''—eventually was echoed by the Crown.

Thus, Bertrand went into the dock of the Central Criminal Court alone.

Two new facts were brought forward at the trial, and Bertrand's counsel, Mr. Dalley, made the very most of both. It was proved that Bertrand, in the three hours which elapsed before a doctor could be found and brought to the wounded man, had staunched the bleeding and bound up Kinder's head skilfully and carefully; also that Kinder, during the days before his death, asked constantly for Bertrand, saying that he would rather have his services than those of any doctor. It was revealed, also, that Kinder supposed his wife to have shot him. Not for a moment did he behave like a suicide who has been baulked of his purpose, or like a man who knows himself to be the victim of accident; which theory the defence continued to put forward.

The Lord Chief Justice dealt with these points in his summing up. He warned the jury; told them that there could not be conceived a case which demanded a more entire absence of prejudice, if justice were to be done.

After the manner of judges, even those most nearly in touch with common life, he bade the jurymen expunge from their minds all recollection of anything they might have read or heard concerning the prisoner, other than such written or spoken statements as had been offered in evidence in that court. This evidence itself, said he, they must weigh; certain parts of it, such as those which "exhibited a state of almost unparalleled wickedness", must not be allowed undue importance. Unless they vigorously strove against preconceptions, the prisoner might be deprived of that justice to which as a citizen he was entitled. He then proceeded in these words:

Regarding him [the prisoner] as the author of the diary, and if you believe this contains the outpourings of his mind, you must not take the picture of this man's mental state as portrayed by the counsel for the defence; for there is before you, not a man, but a fiend, a monster in human shape. Against this conception you will have to struggle; for though steeped in wickedness and malignity scarcely equalled by the Tempter of mankind, the question to be decided by the evidence is, Did he murder Kinder?

Having thus made clear his own opinion of the prisoner, the Lord Chief Justice went on to consider, and dispose of, the accident theory. Supposing, said he, that Kinder did himself press the trigger of the pistol at Bertrand's suggestion; could it be denied that the object and the criminality were the same—the compassing of Kinder's death? Too many circumstances led to the belief that Bertrand wished him to die; it was difficult to assume, in face of these circumstances, that the result of Kinder pulling the trigger was both unexpected and undesired.

The staunching of the blood might be allowed to throw a favourable light upon the prisoner; on the other hand, "had he allowed the man who so wounded himself in his presence to bleed to death, he, as a dentist acquainted with the means to stop haemorrhage, might conceive that he ran some risk." The staunching of the blood, therefore, though inconsistent with the idea of guilt, was not conclusive of innocence.

The defence pleaded that only an innocent man could have prosecuted Jackson for threats which it was in Jackson's power to execute. His Honour disagreed; a man not in full possession of his senses equally might do so, or a man to whom the gratification of revenge meant more than his own safety might do so. "This point, like that of the staunching of the blood, rests on the threshold of your deliberations, and you must get rid of it before proceeding to other matters."

After dealing with the evidence of Jackson, His Honour delivered a further expression of opinion. "There is perhaps nothing so revolting in this case as the fact that this woman [Mrs. Kinder], whilst living with her husband, should be challenged to express her preference for one of two paramours in their presence."

He then passed to the diary, from which he read extracts. "Those passages in which he speaks of what the power of love can perform are pure nonsense, befitting only a madman." His Honour, in fact, laid no great stress upon the evidence offered by the diary, except in so far as it clearly depicted the state of mind of the writer, which was not that of a normal person.

In conclusion, he urged the jury to decide whether Bertrand's own confession (alleged to have been made to his sister) was to be believed, and warned them that confessions were rarely to be relied on. They must set this confession beside other circumstances offered in evidence; and only if they found that these circumstances corroborated the confession, should they allow it any weight. With the usual adjuration to allow the prisoner the benefit of any doubts they might have, His Honour dismissed the jury at one o'clock.

At two o'clock the foreman reappeared, to announce that there was no likelihood of any agreement being reached. His Honour adjourned the court for three hours. At five, and again at six, they were still undecided. An hour later they were locked up for the night. At ten next morning, after a night of argument, the position of the two opposing parties was unchanged. His Honour had no alternative; he dismissed the twelve men who had taken his warnings too closely to heart, and announced that the matter must be re-tried with another jury.

On Friday, just a week after the first trial began, proceedings were recommenced before the same judge. The evidence was heard again, summed up again, and the jury again dismissed to consider it at six in the evening. Two hours later they returned with the unanimous verdict: Guilty.

The prisoner, asked in the usual formula if he had anything to say why sentence of death should not be passed on him, uttered a long and coherent protest; his voice, the newspapers thought, "betrayed no trepidation, and perhaps only a natural weakness." This statement was so long and circumstantial that the Judge, in his final address, felt called upon to reply to it point by point. Said His Honour:

It is no infrequent thing for me to hear protestations of innocence after conviction; but I have never found it consistent with duty, truth, or the interests of society to accord them any serious consideration. Even under the gallows I have known their innocence protested by men of whose guilt I have felt as certain as of anything I have known personally myself, and whose guilt was demonstrated by evidence so clear that no human being possessed of the power of reason could doubt for an instant that the result arrived at had been right. Of course these protestations with many persons go for much, but by those with more experience, equal feeling, more responsibility, who desire to see justice and nothing more, they really pass unheeded.

You are evidently a person of great ability, acuteness, and considerable cunning, with sufficient cleverness to seize upon weak points and make them appear an excuse, which to reflecting persons could be no palliation whatsoever.

You say you are not afraid to die, and I trust you are not, but believe me that in the opinion of the majority of thinking men, wherever this evidence will go, you ought not to hope for forgiveness here.

You say you desire only to clear your character. For whose sake? For the sake of your wife and children. Can it be possible that any human being that has heard what has passed at this trial, who has read the diary, who knows your intercourse with that abandoned woman, supposes that you attempt to clear your character for the sake of your wife and children? How can you, who in the same breath utter a falsehood, be believed in this?

The jury having now pronounced their verdict, I am now at liberty to look at other matters I did not think proper to refer to before. I did not read one line of that to which I am now going to allude. I was informed that Mrs. Kinder might possibly have been tried upon evi-

dence to be given by your wife. Upon inquiry I then
made I found that she had indeed given some information that she was stated to have given to your sister in a
confession, but having been permitted to see you, I believe she has receded from it.

BERTRAND: I have never seen my wife since I have
been in gaol.

HIS LORDSHIP: Then it may be possible she has not
receded from it. I shall feel myself called upon after
your addresses to lay before the public that statement.
If she was not called as a witness with the intelligence
that you possess you must have known that she could
not be called. She has made a statement which, unless
your sister is perjured, positively confirms the verdict
of the jury.

BERTRAND: My sister is perjured.

HIS LORDSHIP: Then the case displays unparalleled
wickedness, but this, the deepest in dye—that a sister,
for no object of her own, should falsely state that your
wife admitted to her that you had shot Kinder. She may
have some remains of affection for your children, and
even for the character of their father, but can I doubt
that your sister spoke the truth when she said she heard
this extraordinary statement from you?

I do not believe you are an insane man, but a perfectly sane man would never have made the declaration
you have made; and I thoroughly believe your sister
when she related this: "I said to his wife, Good God,
has Henry really shot him"; and she answered, "Yes,
he has." Her details, too, are consistent with my idea
of the mode in which the deed was done.

Can anyone doubt the guilt when a man is accused
by his wife and sister, and their statement sustains and
accords with all the probabilities of the case? I hear your

declaration with sorrow and with pain, but I place not the slightest dependence upon it.

I have a greater responsibility than the jury and I declare to you now, before God, I believe you thoroughly guilty, and I have no more doubt of it than that you are before me at this moment. When I first heard the case I did entertain doubts, and I have lain awake hours thinking over the various points involved, and determined if those doubts were not moved not to try you again. But now I have not the slightest doubt of your guilt, and I believe I can demonstrate to any man that you are guilty.

I think it utterly impossible for a rational person to believe that that man shot himself. You say he had intentions. I have had great experience in criminal trials, extending over thirty-two years, and have tried perhaps more cases than any judge in any country, and I have never known a case clearer than your own; nor have I known a single case in which a man who was really determined to kill himself talked about it to his friends. If a man talks of committing suicide, it is almost a proof that he never intends to take his life. Is there the slightest probability that without any temptation and with his pipe in his mouth—having only half an hour before been playing with his child, and just bought oysters for his wife and given them to the servant to prepare for supper—this unfortunate man should, no pistol having been seen in his possession about that time, go into the drawing-room in your presence, in the presence of your wife and his own, and commit a bungling attempt at suicide like that described by you? No person ever heard of such a thing in the annals of crime.

He might have been embarrassed and addicted to drinking. Had he not been a drunkard his wife probably would not have been seduced by Jackson, and you would not have debauched her. If drink did not give the temptation to crime by him, it afforded opportunities for crime in others. All the records of Criminal Courts show repeated instances of crime being committed through the agency of drunkenness—the victim being a drunkard, and affording opportunities for crime against himself. I do not think Kinder was drunk on that day, but whether drunk or sober it is inconceivable that he could have intended to take his life in that bungling, stupid, incredible manner. I find you had every temptation, every motive, for destroying him. You were madly in love with this woman, with a passion eating into your vitals, and you would have committed any crime to have her as your own. Half mad I believe you to be, for you never could have talked as you did, unless there was a partial disturbance of your mind—wild, eccentric, strange to an utterly unprecedented degree, your mind was overshadowed by the influence this unhappy woman had acquired over you.

I hear you say that at the time of writing the impassioned sentences to her, burning with love, you had no other intent than to satisfy the cravings of her romantic feelings. Why, you admit you wrote them as a deep and abandoned hypocrite. I do not believe it. I believe that, maddened by the passion of your attachment to her, you did this terrible deed, and your statements previous were to be accounted for by the idea that in saying his death was likely to occur, when it eventually took place you as his friend would not be looked on with suspicion. I do not make any excuses for Jackson; his conduct was extremely bad. But I feel some sympathy for him, believing that he spoke the truth. I think he deserves punishment, but the law was never meant for a case like his, but for persons who wrote threatening to accuse persons of crimes they never committed, I am satisfied that he believed what he said you did to him in uttering dark, mysterious, dangerous hints, and used expressions justifying him in the belief that you intended to commit the murder; and, therefore, I think the man should be pardoned. He has had sufficient punishment for writing that imprudent letter. But he did not demand money by threatening to accuse you of crime without having grounds for believing you committed it.

You allude to what you call a prejudice against you, yet you must see that it arises in an abhorrence of your proved crimes, and which is the most universal feeling of the country, and this verdict will, I believe, be received with perfect approval.

Nothing can pain a Judge so much as the assumption that a verdict is unjust. I believe you to be guilty, and I shall feel deeper pain than I express if I thought there were anything wrong in the verdict, because I am satisfied you will suffer death. I am sure you deserve the verdict and I am certain in my mind that it is true.

And when you talk about idle words and complain of being spoken of as a fiend, surely when one reads your journal, hears what is said by your sister, by Mrs. Robertson, by Burne, by Bellhouse, and knows why you invited this man to your house, all their testimony uniting and tending the same way, you cannot but be regarded as a fiend. You are not a human being in feeling.

I can speak of you with compassion, because I do not think that you are fully possessed of the mind that God has been pleased to give to almost all of us. On that account alone I feel some sympathy. It is distressing and sad that any father of a family, a man that might be useful in his generation, should die on the scaffold for a crime that makes human nature shudder.

The sentence is that you be taken hence to the place whence you came, and thence, on a day to be named by the Governor in Council, to the place of execution, and at that place to be hanged till your body be dead. If you are to find mercy, as I hope you will, seek it elsewhere, but from no human tribunal.

But His Honour's certainty of the prisoner's guilt, and his desire to save time, led him into an impropriety. To avoid calling again every witness who had spoken at the first trial, the Chief Justice, during the course of the second trial, read to the jury from his own notes certain items of evidence. This had been done, in fact, at the instance of the prisoner himself, who, weary with repetitions, had pleaded that His Honour should take every means to bring his ordeal soon to an end. But the Supreme Court, to which appeal was immediately made, found this a point of great significance, and the four judges' opinions were equally divided as to whether or no there had been a mistrial. It was argued for four days; the result of a similar inquiry in England, which might afford a precedent, was ascertained by letter and telegram; and as a result the Court ordered that the verdict should be vacated the record; the prisoner meanwhile being held in custody to await his third trial at the next sittings of the Supreme Court in its criminal jurisdiction, to be held in the following May.

The Legislative Assembly of New South Wales then took up the affair. The behaviour and competence of the Chief Justice, with one of the other judges of the Supreme Court, offered matter for questions. The Government was implored, on the one hand to appeal to the Privy Council, and, alternatively, begged not to bring the judicature of the colony into disrepute by so doing. A magnificent public quarrel was blowing up, when Bertrand himself, to use one of his own phrases, cut the knot. The doctors at long last gave him a certificate of madness, and he was removed from Darlinghurst to the prison for criminal lunatics at Parramatta.

X

From the point of view of a reader of detection stories, this is an unsatisfactory crime. The murderer was insane, and the purist in these matters prefers a murderer who is *compos mentis*; the chain of logical deduction should not, he thinks, clank to a madman's fandango. It is a crime which defies all the canons. Premeditated, it yet was committed before a cloud of witness; even, one of these had been brought to the spot marked with a cross deliberately, and against her will, by the chief performer. Its object was to obtain sole possession of a woman who had already yielded to the criminal, and was, in the words of his associate, "as good as a wife to him". It was discovered, not through any process of suspicion and inquiry, but owing to the indiscretion of the man who had actually bluffed a coroner's jury into a verdict of suicide, but who, even to save his neck, could not hold his tongue. The police had only to listen, to search, and, when they had found Bertrand's letters and diary, to present their case.

That Bertrand did kill Henry Kinder is indisputable. The amateur of crime, disgusted with the whole flamboyantly silly proceeding, finds a stimulus to curiosity at one point only. By what means was Henry Kinder killed? The coroner's jury brought in a verdict of death by shooting. The post-mortem finding, death from haemorrhage and shock, was nothing more than a variation upon the jury's theme.

Nor is it easy to pick out the truth from Bertrand's grim-
aces and boasts. Still, the puzzling facts may be compared
with his fantasies to afford matter for a guess.

Kinder did not die until four days after he was wounded
by the discharge of Bertrand's pistol; was, indeed, in a fair
way to recover from the wound which broke his jaw and
tore off most of his ear. He died suddenly, after Jane Bertrand had given him a glass of milk. This, Jane's own
story, comes at second-hand; but Mrs. Robertson testified
to hearing Bertrand crying out in his fit, the night before
Kinder died: "Bring the milk and mix the poison." In
Bertrand's possession were found two vegetable poisons,
aconite and belladonna, both of a nature to defy the chemist who assisted at the investigation of Kinder's exhumed
body.

To quote Dr. Ainsworth Mitchell, editor of *The Analyst*:
"Medical criminals have often banked upon difficulties
likely to be experienced in detecting vegetable alkaloids."
The test for aconitine was not perfected until later, when
Dr. Stevenson, by a series of experiments upon mice, established its presence in the body of Dr. Lamson's victim.
Even so, the defence in that famous case suggested the
possibility that effects attributed to aconitine might also
have been caused by some substance of an alkaloidal nature formed in the decomposition of animal matter. Belladonna, more familiar nowadays under the name of its
active principle, atropine, was, and is, equally as elusive.
Both these poisons were (quite legitimately) in Bertrand's
possession; and Bertrand was a dentist, with enough general medical knowledge to call for comment from the
judge. He may be allowed, for purposes of argument, to
rank as a medical criminal. It is, for the detection story
reader, a problem incapable of solution; hardly a problem
at all, but rather a question of looking upon this picture

and on this, and making a choice of suspicions. On the one hand, a man succumbs to the shock of a wound not neccessarily fatal, as a result of previous known excesses in drink, by which his resistance has been weakened. "It would shorten anybody's days." On the other hand, a murderer, already over the edge of sanity, hears that the victim whose death has been for weeks the main concern of his imagination is about to recover. He has poisons at hand, and an instrument; his wife, dazed, frightened, unable to refuse to perform his will. He is aware, in some convolution of his uneasy brain, that vegetable alkaloids take a lot of tracing in a dead man's body.

Penny plain, twopence coloured. There is, and can be now no proof; as young Osric says, nothing neither way. But to the writer, as to the reader of detection stories, the second alternative is the more acceptable of the two.

XI

The main interest of this trial, apart from those purely legal complications which eventually brought about an appeal to the Privy Council, lies in the picture it offers of a lunatic murderer going about his business unhampered by sane persons to whom he had confided his purpose. "People don't do these things," the citizens of Sydney told each other; men capable of earning a fair living and playing a good game of cards are not to be suspected of homicidal tendencies. They took no steps, therefore, to restrain the young dentist who roared like a tiger when yawning in the street, who strolled Sydney by night dressed as a woman, vowed he could raise ghosts, and in the midst of a rubber of whist announced, with appropriate gesture, that he was the personal devil.

De Fries, Jackson, and Burne seem to have made no

effort to get a doctor to Bertrand, or, when Kinder died, to inform the police of what they knew. De Fries did indeed plead with Bertrand for better treatment of his wife, and told Mrs. Robertson that he must be insane to go on as he did. But "he said it in a jocular manner." Burne, a party to all his employer's plans, buying pistols for him, rowing with him while the murderous tomahawk swung under his coat, held his tongue, would not speak until he was subpœnaed, even after Bertrand had been gaoled on another charge. He was twenty years old, and by no means unsophisticated, having played 'juvenile business' at the Victoria Theatre before he came to the dentist as assistant. It is inconceivable that, after the first expedition in the boat, he should not have perceived Bertrand's mental condition. Having accompanied him on three of these ventures and bought the pistols, it is understandable that he should then be afraid to speak. But how came he to undertake such commissions? How came he to remain in that equivocal employment at all? Fear accounts for some part of his conduct; for the rest we must hold responsible the reluctance of the normal human being to suppose that a man with whom he is in daily contact, and from whom he takes orders, is not right in his mind.

It is evident from the behaviour of these people that in many ways Bertrand could tell a hawk from a handsaw still; he was but mad nor'-nor'-west. His journal speaks rationally of money matters, and gives a shrewd picture of Mr. Wood, Helen Kinder's shiftless father, who, having been told how matters stood between his daughter and the dentist, attempted to make capital out of his knowledge. His brutalities to poor Jane were kept secret, though he thrashed her with a whip and assaulted her with a penknife, after which last incident Jane showed her sister-in-law a pair of corsets soaked with blood. His mother-in law, who visited the house often, was able to swear in court that he was very kind to her daughter, and by no means a man of strange manners and habits. Bellhouse, told the facts of the murder by Bertrand, casually, after a game of cards, could not make up his mind to believe that what he had heard was the truth, and lay awake all night debating the question. It would seem that in general Bertrand's manner was normal enough; so that it must have been shocking to hear him offer, over the whist-table, to raise the ghost of the man he had killed; or to look up from that most innocent of occupations, the bathing of a baby, and be told: "Kinder did not shoot himself, I shot him."

The heroine of the story, Ellen Kinder, makes no such extraordinary impression upon the mind; her behaviour rouses no question. She was a hearty, handsome, practical woman, fond of her pleasures, combining promiscuity with a genuine affection and care for her children. It is easy enough to believe that she yielded to Bertrand from fear; yet her imagination was not of a quality to tell her that the threats he was for ever making against her husband might one day come to action. The passion in her letters has in it a tang of theatre and of the expected. Perhaps this is always so; perhaps the true language of persons moved by great excitement is that of melodrama. "I had rather see you dead at my feet"; "I cannot live without seeing you"; "I shall go mad at the thought of our meeting"—all these are stock phrases which may stand for the expression of genuine as of false emotion. But the voice of the real Ellen Kinder is not to be heard in them. Rather she comes alive in such phrases as these, taken at random from her letters to her lover:

"Papa quite expects me to make a good match one of these days. I tell him I would not give thanks for the best man living, if I could make my own living."

"I feel my position very much, as I know how little

we are able to afford the extra expense we must be at. If there were anything I could do to make it up I should not mind, but there is absolutely nothing. I do not know how things are to go on if it were not for the children."

"We are almost decided to take an hotel here, but on second thought I do not care much for it. I should not mind a respectable house in Sydney, but this is such a bad place. This is, oh, dreadfully matter of fact, dear dear love, but it is necessary, therefore I hope you will not mind it."

"You see, deary, an hotel is such a public affair, that my position would be noticeable directly. I should not like to be in a public, and I know that you would not like for me to be a disgrace to everyone connected with me."

"I must not forget to thank you for seeing about my business. I should like to get into a first-rate establishment for a few weeks to learn dressmaking, as a really good one would do well here. In that case, there is no place like Sydney; but, darling, I leave myself entirely in your hands—feeling, love, you will do everything for the best."

It is not surprising after all these protestations to note that the first employment found by Mrs. Kinder after her acquittal was in an hotel. She returned to New Zealand, whence she had come three years before; a public-house keeper with some sense of the value of advertisement engaged her as barmaid, in which position she was completely successful. Almost at once, however, she married again, and, for all anyone at this date can tell, died full of years and highly respected.

PART II

Constance Kent

by John Rhode

THE name of Constance Kent and the nature of the extra-ordinary crime to which she eventually confessed are familiar to almost everybody. For this reason I do not propose to give a detailed description of the crime itself. To those who wish to peruse it more fully, many sources are available.[1] My present purpose is to deal with the curious personality of the criminal herself in the light of information which has become available during the past few years.

A brief résumé of the crime may, however, be found convenient. Mr. Samuel Saville Kent had at one time been in business in the City of London. About 1834 he obtained the appointment of Sub-Inspector of Factories for the West of England, which was then the important centre of the cloth trade. In the year 1860 he was living at Road Hill House, on the border of Somerset and Wiltshire. The house

[1] Among these I may perhaps be permitted to mention my *The Case of Constance Kent*, in the Famous Trials Series. London, Geoffrey Bles, 1928.

stands back from the road, by which it is approached by a carriage drive. It is of a fair size, and then stood in about half an acre of ground laid out as lawn, shrubbery, kitchen-garden and flower-garden. On the right-hand side of the house, looking from the drive, was a spacious paved court-yard communicating with the kitchen and domestic offices on the one side, and on the other with the kitchen-garden. Two pairs of large and high gates opened out of the yard, one pair into a lane running parallel to the side of the house, the other into the carriage drive. Outside the latter gates and to the right of them, was a small shrubbery, concealing a detached earth-closet. At the period of the crime this closet was rarely used, the house having been fitted with inside sanitation.

On the evening of Friday, June 29, 1860, the house was occupied by twelve individuals. These were Mr. Kent; his second wife, who was then expecting a confinement; three daughters: Mary Ann, Elizabeth and Constance; and a son, William, of Mr. Kent's first marriage. Two daughters, Mary Amelia and Emilie, and a son, Francis Saville, of Mr. Kent's second marriage. The cook, the housemaid and the nurse, by name Elizabeth Gough. On this partic-ular evening there was no deviation from the routine of the house. Mr. and Mrs. Kent slept in a room on the first floor. This room was in the front of the house. Separated from it by a fairly wide passage at the end of which was a dressing-room, was the nursery. In the nursery slept Elizabeth Gough and the two younger children of the sec-ond marriage: Francis Saville, aged four, and Emilie, aged two. Mary Amelia, eldest child of the second marriage, slept in the room occupied by Mr. and Mrs. Kent. The remaining rooms on the first floor were unoccupied. On the second floor the two eldest daughters of the first mar-riage, Mary Ann and Elizabeth, slept together in the room above that occupied by Mr. and Mrs. Kent. Constance Kent slept alone in the adjoining room, above the passage and the dressing-room. The cook and housemaid slept together in the room adjoining hers above the nursery. It is worthy of remark that the partitions between these three rooms were very thin and there is abundant evidence that sounds originating in one room could be heard in that next door. On this floor, looking out at the back of the house, was the room occupied by William Kent. Two other rooms were unoccupied.

At the usual hour, which was half-past seven, Elizabeth Gough put the youngest child Emilie to bed in the nursery. Half an hour later she put Francis Saville to bed, also in the nursery. The remainder of the family retired in rotation. Before the cook went to bed she fastened and secured the domestic offices. Similarly, before she went to bed, the housemaid fastened and secured the remainder of the ground floor, including a french window in the drawing-room which looked out towards the back of the house. The nurse went to bed a little before eleven, leaving Mr. and Mrs. Kent in the dining-room. She was some time in the nursery before she undressed, having her supper and tidying up. While she was thus occupied Mrs. Kent came into the room and looked at the children asleep in bed. Mrs. Kent then went downstairs and came up to bed a few minutes later. Until this moment the nursery door had been open in order that the nurse might hear any sound from the child who was sleeping in the Kents' room. As she went to bed, Mrs. Kent shut this door. Mr. Kent was the last to retire. He went to bed a little before midnight, having, according to his own subsequent statement, examined all the fastenings in the house.

At five o'clock the next morning the nurse awoke. She looked at Francis' cot and found that he was no longer there. This occasioned her no surprise at the time. She supposed that during the night Mrs. Kent had heard the child crying and had come in and removed him to her own room. This supposition was strengthened by the fact that the bedclothes of the cot had been neatly re-arranged. The nurse then went to sleep again.

At a quarter or twenty minutes to seven, the nurse went into Mrs. Kent's room. Supposing that Mrs. Kent had both Mary Amelia and Francis, her object was to ask for one of them so that she might dress it. She knocked twice on the door but obtained no answer, and in view of Mrs. Kent's condition thought it better to disturb her no further. However, she made another attempt at a quarter-past seven, when she found Mrs. Kent dressed in her dressing-gown. On that occasion Mrs. Kent told her that she had not seen the child. The nurse then went upstairs to the second floor to make inquiries of Mary Ann and Elizabeth. At the time of Constance Kent's appearance before the magistrates, the nurse gave the following evidence upon this point:

> Miss Constance slept in a room which is between where her two sisters sleep and where the cook and housemaid sleep. The partition between them is very thin. You can even hear a paper rustling in either room. When I went to inquire of the Misses Kent the prisoner came to the door. I observed nothing unusual in her manner at the time.[1]

Meanwhile the housemaid had made a significant discovery. This is best described in her own words.[2]

---

[1] Quoted from a contemporary report in the *Somerset and Wilts Journal*.

[2] This statement had been made at the inquest. It is quoted from the *Somerset and Wilts Journal*.

On Friday evening I fastened the door and shutters in the drawing-room as usual. I am positive that I did so. I have no doubt in the matter whatever. The shutters fasten with iron bars and each has two brass bolts besides. That was all made secure on Friday evening. The door has a bolt and a lock and I bolted it and turned the key of the lock, so that anyone coming from the house would have the power of unfastening the door and windows and anyone coming in from the outside must smash the windows and then would not be able to open the shutters without using a centre bit or making a hole in the shutters. On Friday evening I retired to bed about a quarter to eleven and rose about five minutes past six on Saturday morning. Mr. Kent was the last person who went to bed that evening. He is in the habit of staying till the last.

When I came down in the morning, I saw that the drawing-room door was a little open, the bolt was back and the lock turned. There was no displacement of the furniture in the room. Of the windows, the lower shutters were open, the bolts being back and the window slightly open. There was no blood, footmarks or displacement in the room.

Search within the house having proved unavailing, the alarm was given. Mr. Kent himself took horse and started for Trowbridge, some five miles away, to inform the superintendent of police. The neighbours were called into assist the search. Two of these found the missing child. His body was in the earth-closet beside the shrubbery. The throat had been cut, almost severing the head from the body, and there was a deep wound in the breast. The body was wrapped in a bloodstained blanket which had been taken from its cot. Mr. Kent was recalled and a doctor was summoned. On his arrival he, Dr. Parsons, saw that the child had been dead at least five hours. The consensus of medical opinion subsequently agreed that death must have taken place about 1 a.m. on Saturday morning.

The investigation into the crime was at first carried out without the slightest attempt at method. Mr. Henry Rhodes, in his *Some Persons Unknown*[1] says:

> In this affair, the search seems to have been carried out with great negligence and indiscriminately by the police and the neighbours, while the interrogation of the members of the family left a great deal to be desired. Scientific methods, whether in the matter of taking evidence or in the discovery of clues, were not then popular.

This was no exaggeration. The local constable, though an early visitor to the scene, took no steps to preserve such clues as might exist. He seems to have departed almost immediately to inform his superiors. Meanwhile, the excited villagers took every advantage of their opportunity. To quote a contemporary account:[2]

> The house and premises were then minutely searched. Male and female searchers in the course of the day examined every individual and every room, box and water-closet about the place, emptied the earth-closet and scoured the vicinity, but without finding any knife or garment stained with blood, or any article to afford the least clue, except a piece of flannel apparently worn as

[1]London, John Murray, 1931.
[2]In the *Somerset and Wilts Journal*.

a chest protector which was underneath the child's body stained with blood.

It was hardly to be expected that the zeal of these amateurs should be rewarded by success.

The inquest was held upon the following Monday. The foreman of the jury was a local parson, a close friend of Mr. Kent and his family. He seems to have done his best to shield the family from any breath of the suspicions which had already been aroused. The coroner seems to have sympathized with his attitude. No member of the family was called upon to give evidence until a protest was made by a majority of the jury. The coroner reluctantly acceded to their request. He said:

I must say, I do not see what end will be answered by it. They will only confirm what we have already heard and say they know no more about it. But it is the wish of the majority of the jury, it must be done.

The jury then requested that Constance and William Kent might be examined. The evidence given by Constance Kent on this occasion will be considered later. The coroner then recommended the jury to record a verdict of murder by some person or persons unknown. The majority of the jurymen were not inclined to accept this advice, but were over-ruled by their foreman. This verdict was actually returned after the inquest had lasted five hours—an hour and a half of which, it is stated, were spent by the jury in examining the body.

The next step in the investigation of the crime was an inquiry by the Trowbridge Bench, which had for its ostensible purpose the examination of witnesses. This inquiry opened on July 9th and was continued at intervals until the 27th. During this period one of the magistrates approached the Home Secretary and, as a result, Inspector Whicher, an officer of Scotland Yard, was sent to Road to assist in the investigations.

Whicher was an extremely able man. He did not arrive on the scene until a fortnight after the crime had been committed, but he set to work methodically to examine such clues as still remained. As a result he accumulated evidence which seemed to him to point to Constance Kent as the culprit. At his instance she was arrested. After being in custody for a week, she appeared before the magistrate and was triumphantly acquitted. Local opinion was not favourable to Whicher. In its eyes Constance Kent had been martyred in the cause of officialdom. Loud applause greeted the announcement of the chairman of the Bench that the prisoner should be released on her father becoming bound for her on £200, to appear when called upon.

Whicher returned to London to be overwhelmed with censure for arresting an innocent girl. But none the less he remained convinced of her guilt. On November 23rd of the same year he wrote to the Chief Superintendent of the Bristol police upon the subject. In the course of this letter he said:

> Now, in my opinion, if there was ever one man to be pitied or who has been more calumniated than another, that unfortunate man is Mr. Kent. It was bad enough to have his darling child cruelly murdered, but to be branded as the murderer is far worse, and, according to the present state of public opinion, he will be so branded till the day of his death unless a confession is made by the person whom I firmly believe committed the deed. I have little doubt that the confession would have been

made if Miss Constance had been remanded for another week.

The next sensation connected with the case was an extraordinary one. An unemployed mason who eventually gave his name as John Edmond Gagg, accosted a railway policeman at Wolverton station in Buckinghamshire and confessed to the crime. He was taken to Trowbridge and there examined by the magistrate. Short examination showed that never in his life had he been to Road and that he was many miles away at the commission of the crime.

The next step was the opening of an inquiry by Mr. Slack, a solicitor practising in Bath. Mr. Slack refused to divulge by which authority he acted. All he would say was that "those who instructed him had the authority by the Home Office for so doing." His inquiry opened on September 17th and, apparently as the result of it, the local police took action. Elizabeth Gough had left Mr. Kent's service by this time and had gone to her home at Isleworth. She was there arrested, brought to Trowbridge, and formally charged with the murder of Francis Saville Kent. At her appearance before the magistrate no further evidence was produced. The Bench had no option but to release her. The remarks of the chairman on this occasion are interesting:

The magistrate has determined on not committing the prisoner for trial although there was a case of grave suspicion against her, and material had been adduced which with additions might hereafter be brought to bear against her. They would bind her accordingly to appear when called on in two sureties of £50 each.

On November 3rd one of the magistrates, Mr. Saunders, opened an inquiry upon his own account. He examined a number of witnesses, and in spite of, or perhaps because of, the irregularity of his proceedings he elicited certain very curious facts. For this reason the record of his proceedings is worthy of perusal in spite of its farcical nature.[1] But it led to no definite results and was finally abandoned.

Meanwhile Mr. Slack had not been idle. On November 26th an application was made by the Attorney-General at the Court of Queen's Bench before the Lord Chief Justice for a writ for a better inquest on the body of Francis Saville Kent. The Solicitor-General appeared on behalf of the writ, and Sir Fitzroy Kelly represented the coroner in opposing it. The latter gained the day. The Lord Chief Justice said that the only grounds upon which the application rested was the allegation of misconduct on the part of the coroner, in the single instance of his not accepting the offer spontaneously made by the solicitor of Mr. Kent and not examining Mr. Kent. His Lordship said he thought the coroner would have exercised the sounder discretion if he had accepted the offer, but it was not for a mere error of judgment that this court would set aside an inquisition demanded by a coroner's jury. If there had been judicial misconduct of a nature to justify the court to set aside the inquisition, it would still be a question whether that should be done and a new inquisition issued, when it was seen what the object was, viz., to examine those among whom the guilt of the crime necessarily rested, to ascertain from

[1] A full account of Mr. Saunders' proceedings may be found in a book entitled *The Great Crime of 1860*, published in 1861 by E. Marlborough and Co., London. The author of this book was Mr. Stapleton, a surgeon who assisted at the post-mortem on the body of the murdered child, and who was apparently on terms of intimacy with the Kent family. The book is now, unfortunately, out of print.

their separate depositions which of whom had committed the crime. That would not be a proper exercise of the jurisdiction of this court. To issue such an inquisition to obtain evidence against them for that was an object which the law would not sanction. The rule was discharged.

After this the investigation was abandoned. Mr. Kent and his family left Road Hill House and settled at Weston-super-Mare. The contents were sold by auction, and an enormous crowd attended the sale. The object of the members of the crowd was not to bid but to inspect the earth-closet. It is recorded that

> Superintendent Foley was often requested to gratify the eager curiosity of the visitors by showing it. The spots of blood on the floor are still there, and it was strange to see young and fashionably dressed ladies seeking to learn every particular and see every spot connected with the murder.[1]

Four years later, on April 25, 1865, Constance Kent surrendered herself at Bow Street Police Court and confessed to the murder of Francis Saville Kent.

Constance Kent was the ninth child of Samuel Saville Kent's first marriage. In 1829 Mr. Kent had married Mary Ann Winder, and by her had ten children, five of whom died shortly after birth. At the date of the crime four of these children were still living, Mary Ann, Elizabeth, Constance, and William. Constance had been born at Sidmouth in February 1844. It is alleged[2] by Dr Stapleton, who subsequently became a friend of the family, that her mother had exhibited symptoms of insanity as early as

[1] *Somerset and Wilts Journal.*
[2] Stapleton, *op. cit.*

1836. According to his account, these symptoms were not very serious. He says, however, that "the early treatment of Mrs. Kent appears to have been most lamentably deficient and abortive."

Six years later, however, Mr. Kent decided to employ a capable woman to superintend the children and the household. But the fact of Mrs. Kent's insanity has been questioned. A single quotation[1] will suffice to exemplify the doubt which has been thrown upon the matter.

Was Mrs. Kent insane? Her two eldest daughters always vehemently denied it. No act has ever been mentioned to prove it. The second governess, who was employed for the education of the two eldest daughters, arrived about the time of John's birth in 1842. She was a pretty, very capable woman. Considering Mrs. Kent's frequent confinements, also several miscarriages, and that servants took advantage of the circumstances, was it anything out of the way that Mr. Kent was only too glad to find someone willing and able to superintend the menage? Many wives are incompetent or unwilling as housekeepers, but they are not therefore deemed insane. As Mr. Kent only ceased to live with her about two years later, did he then consider her so?

[1] This is from a remarkable document, addressed to the author shortly after the publication of his *The Case of Constance Kent*, and now deposited in the library of the Detection Club, London. It is dated February 1929, and was posted in Sydney, New South Wales. Though unsigned, it contains ample internal evidence of having been written, if not by Constance Kent herself, at least by some person having a very intimate knowledge of her childhood and history. Although anonymous, the wording of this document is sufficiently convincing to allow its quotation, not necessarily in support of facts, but as shedding light upon the strange character of Constance Kent. In subsequent notes it will be cited as the Sydney document.

When Constance was four years old the family moved to Walton, between Clevedon and Portishead in Somersetshire. They remained here four years, and in March 1852 moved once more, this time to Baynton House, near Corsham in Wiltshire. A few weeks after this move Mrs. Kent died. In August 1853 Mr. Kent took as his second wife the governess-housekeeper, Miss Pratt. In 1855 the family moved to Road Hill House, where the four children of the second marriage were born. The second of these was Francis Saville, who was born in August 1856.

At the time of Francis' birth, Constance was twelve, and from various sources something may be gathered of her childhood. Mr. Stapleton says:[1]

For many months after her birth great apprehensions were entertained that Constance would share the fate of the four previous children of Mrs. Kent. That she struggled through the feebleness of her early infancy is chiefly due to the devotion and personal attention of Miss Pratt, by whom she was fed, nursed and waited upon for months. By degrees her bodily constitution assumed that healthy development and growth which has bestowed on her the contour and command of a powerful physique. As she grew up Constance manifested a strong, obstinate and determined will, and her conduct even as a little child gave evidence of an irritable and impassioned nature.

The document already quoted[2] draws a vivid picture of the relations between Constance and Miss Pratt.

[1] *Op. cit.*
[2] The Sydney document.

The governess had made a great pet of Constance and was very fond of her, but soon trouble began. The governess had a theory that once a child said a letter or spelt a word right it could not forget it, and she conscientiously believed that it was her duty to treat any lapse as obstinacy. The letter H gave Constance many hours of confinement in a room where she listened longingly to the music and the sights of the lawn outside. When words were to be mastered punishments became more severe. Days were spent shut up in a room with dry bread and milk and water for tea. At other times she would be stood up in a corner of the hall sobbing, "I want to be good, I do, I do," till she came to the conclusion that goodness was impossible for a child and that she could only hope to grow up quickly as grown-ups were never naughty. At times she gave way to furious fits of temper and was locked away in a distant room and sometimes in a cellar that her noise might not annoy people.

Constance did not take her punishments very seriously, but generally managed to get some amusement out of them. Once after being particularly provocative and passionate, the governess put her down in a dark wine cellar. She fell on a heap of straw and fancied herself in the dungeon of a great castle, a prisoner taken in a battle fighting for Bonnie Prince Charlie and to be taken to the block next morning. When the governess unlocked the door and told her to come up she was looking rather pleased over her fancies. The governess asked her what she was smiling about: "Oh," she said, "only the funny rats."

"What rats?" said the governess, who did not know there were any there.

"They do not hurt me. Only dance and play about."

After that, to her disappointment she was shut in the beer cellar, a light room but with a window too high to look out of. She managed to pull the spigot out of a cask of beer. After that, she was locked up in one of two spare rooms at the end of the vestibule, shut off by double doors. She liked the big room, for it had a large four-poster bed she could climb about, but the little room was dreary. The rooms had a legend attached to them and were said to be haunted on a certain date when a blue fire burned in the fireplace.

At one time at Baynton House Constance's place of punishment was in one of the empty garrets. The house was built in the shape of an E and there was a parapet round the best part of the house. She used to climb out of the window and up the bend to the top of the roof and slide down the other side. She tied an old fur across her chest to act the monkey and call it playing Cromwell. To return she got through the window of another garret. The governess was puzzled at always finding the door unlocked with the key left in. The servants were questioned, but of course knew nothing. One day she found Constance and her brother out on the ledge, and told them not to do it as it was dangerous. Next time when she did climb out she found the window fastened. She could not climb back the way she came, but just where the parapet ended was the window of a room where the groom slept. She reached across and climbed through, and though she upset and broke a jug on the washstand, the cat got the credit for this. Afterwards, she heard that her father did not approve of the window being fastened to trap her, and said that when unruly she could be shut in the study, the room where her father wrote and kept his papers. Being on the ground floor she easily got out of the window and passed her

time climbing the trees in the shrubbery, also displaying
a very cruel disposition by impaling slugs and snails on
sticks in trees, calling these crucifixions. The affection
between Constance and the governess no longer existed.

Meanwhile, Miss Pratt's position in the household had
become the subject of unfavourable comment. Mr. Kent's
eldest surviving son, Edward, nine years older than Constance, seems to have been the first to express disapproval.
It is reported that one morning when he was at home at
Sidmouth on his holidays, he met his father coming out of
the governess's room which happened to be next to his. A
scene took place between father and son, as a result of
which the latter was promptly sent back to school. After
this Edward was very rarely at home. He took to the sea
as a profession, and died at Havana of yellow fever in
1858.

At this time Constance was too young to notice anything
of this. But as she grew up her childish recollections began
to assume significance. She realized that there had been
something mysterious about the treatment of her mother.

Why did her mother, when speaking to her, often call
herself, your poor mamma, which the governess said
was silly? Why was the governess taken out for drives
and her mother never? Why was her father in the library
with the governess while the rest of the family was with
her mother? She remembered many little incidents
which seemed strange. One was during a thunderstorm,
when the governess acted as though she were frightened
and rushed over to her father who drew her down on his
knee and kissed her. The governess exclaimed: ''Oh,
not before the child!'' Though her mother seemed to

feel being placed in the background, why did she not resent it and assert herself?[1]

The relations between Mr. Kent and the governess can only be conjectural and they do not concern us directly. But in the light of subsequent events, we are bound to consider the effect of them upon a child of the passionate nature of Constance. An antagonism developed between the two, which increased after Mr. Kent's second marriage. By this time her stepmother seems to have given Constance up in despair, and made no attempt to propitiate her. In any case, Constance would have been a difficult child to propitiate if contemporary accounts of her are to be believed. On the other hand, the second Mrs. Kent seems to have shown very little sympathy with the children of the first family. These were kept under constant surveillance and their friendships very strictly regulated. On one occasion the two eldest girls made friends with the daughters of two neighbouring families, but as these families showed a reluctance to call upon the Kents, probably owing to their disapproval of Mrs. Kent, orders were issued that these friendships must cease and the prohibition was extended to the younger children.

One day when Constance and her brother were supposed to be attending to their little garden behind the shrubbery, they heard some merry laughter from the neighbouring garden. They went to the hedge and looked over longingly at the children playing with visitors. They were invited to join, but were afraid. They were seen and their disobedience punished. The little gardens were uprooted and trampled down. Constance made some futile

[1]The Sydney document.

efforts to revive hers. No pets were allowed, two little tropical birds sent by the eldest son to his sisters were confined to a cold back room and died.

There was no evidence of direct cruelty on the part of the second Mrs. Kent towards Constance. She seems to have misunderstood the child's nature and Constance, in turn, was undoubtedly resentful of authority. At school she was perpetually in trouble, mainly through the deliberate perverseness of her attitude. She became, apparently as the result of her behaviour, the odd man out of the family. She certainly seems to have been a difficult child to get on with.

We are told[1] that she did not always come home for holidays. On one occasion when she did, no one took any notice. She might just have come in from a walk. She was sitting at a window rather disconsolately when her step-mother wanted her to do some mending. She refused, and her stepmother said:

"Do you know that only for me you would have remained at school? When I said you were coming one of your sisters exclaimed: 'What, that tiresome girl!' So you see, they do not want you."

As a result of this kind of treatment she made up her mind that she was not wanted and that everyone was against her. She formed, for a girl of her age and period, the most extraordinary resolution. This was nothing less than to dress up as a boy and run away to sea. She had acquired considerable influence over her brother, William, who was a year younger than she was. Mr. Stapleton's account[2] of her attempt to put her resolution into practice may well be quoted:

---

[1]The Sydney document.
[2]*Op. cit.*

In the escapade, which was planned and executed by
Constance, her younger brother William seems to have
been a passive and compliant agent in his sister's hands.
During the holidays, June 1856, they had been at home
from school together. Their holidays had already ex-
pired, but they had been kept at home for a few days
longer pending the return of their father from an absence on business in Devonshire. There is no evidence
to show that any recent or particular fracas had happened during Mr. Kent's absence. But at all events, in
the afternoon of the day before Mr. Kent's return, Constance and William were not to be found. An alarm was
at once raised. Search was made but without success.

Now comes rather a curious point. Constance needed a
safe hiding-place for her own purposes. The earth-closet
in the shrubbery occurred to her, whether or not for the
first time it is impossible to say. We may continue the
story in Mr. Stapleton's own words:

After lunch on the day she left home, she went down
to the closet in the shrubbery, put on some old clothes
of her brother William's which she had secreted and
mended, and cut off her hair, which she flung with her
own clothes into the vault of the closet. She then started
with her brother on a walk of ten miles to Bath, where
they arrived in the evening. They went to the Greyhound
Hotel where they asked for beds.

Their appearance excited the suspicions of the landlady, and they were questioned by her. Constance was
very self-possessed and even insolent in her manner and
language. William soon broke down and burst into tears.
He was placed in bed at the inn, and as nothing could
be done with Constance, the police were called in and

she was given into custody for the night. She allowed herself to be separated from her brother, and was taken to the Central Police Station where she spent the night in the common detention room, maintaining the most resolute bearing and a determined silence as to her history. Early in the morning their father's servant discovered them and took them home. Upon Mr. Kent's return the same day, William at once expressed the greatest sorrow and contrition and sobbed bitterly. Constance for many days continued in solitude and gave no evidence of regret or shame at her conduct. At last she said she wished to be independent, and her object appears to have been to reach Bristol and to leave England with her brother.

That a girl of twelve should have behaved with so much resolution is almost incredible. The incident, however, is confirmed from many other sources. Constance possessed both shrewdness and determination, and was not likely to let any consideration whatever stand in her way. Shortly after this, she was sent to another school, kept by relatives of the second Mrs. Kent. It was hoped, perhaps, that they would be able to tame the intractable child. But all efforts in this direction failed. She took a delight in scandalizing her new teachers, and it would appear that after some months they refused to take charge of her any longer. Yet another attempt was made. Constance was sent as a boarder to Beckington, a village within a mile or two of the Kents' house. Here she remained off and on until shortly before the commission of the crime.

It is now time to consider the attitude adopted by Constance during the investigations which followed the crime. Her first appearance was as a witness at the inquest on July 2nd. On this occasion she is described as "a robust

young lady, rather tall for her age", and we are told "that
she gave her evidence in a subdued but audible tone, without betraying any special emotion, her eyes fixed on the
ground".[1] Answering the questions of the coroner she declared that she knew nothing about this affair until her
brother was found. About half-past ten on Friday night
she had gone to bed and she knew nothing until after
eleven o'clock. She generally slept soundly. She did not
leave her bed during the night. She did not know of anyone having any spite against the boy. There had been no
disagreement in the house, and she was not aware of anyone owing any grudge against the deceased. The nurse had
always been kind and attentive to him. On Saturday morning she heard that he was dead. She was then getting up.

We have already seen that the news reached her through
the nurse's visit to her sisters' room which was next door
to her own.

The next public appearance of Constance was in the
dock before the Trowbridge magistrates after her arrest by
Inspector Whicher. Whicher had put into practice the prin-
ciples of sound detection. He had arrived at Constance's
guilt by simple deduction. How he had done so, may
shortly be stated in his own words.[2]

Whoever did the deed, doubtless did it in their night-
clothes. When Constance Kent went to bed that night
she had three nightdresses belonging to her in the house.
After the murder she had but two. What then became
of the third? It was not lost in the wash as it was so
craftily endeavoured to make it appear, but it was lost

[1]*Somerset and Wilts Journal.*
[2]In a letter written by him on November 23, 1860, to the Chief Superintendent of the Bristol Police.

in some other way. Where is it, then, and what became
of it?

The evidence on the subject of this nightdress must be
given at some length. Sarah Cox, the housemaid, deposed
as follows.[1]

    I had to collect dirty linen from the room on Monday
morning. That of Miss Constance is generally thrown
down either in the room or on the landing, some of it
on Sunday and some of it on Monday. It was so on this
occasion, Monday, July 2nd. I found a nightdress of
hers on the landing on Monday morning, and took it
down with the rest to the lumber-room on the first floor
to sort it out. I then called Miss Kent to come and put
the number on the book. [This Miss Kent was Mary
Ann, the eldest daughter.] I perfectly remember putting
this nightdress of Miss Constance's in the basket after
the murder. I left the basket in the lumber-room when
I went down to the inquest about eleven o'clock with
the nurse. Mr. and Mrs. Kent, the three young ladies,
Master Kent, the young children, and the cook remained in the house. The baskets were covered up with
the kitchen tablecloth and Mrs. Kent's dress, and the
lumber-room was not locked. The laundress was to
come for them about twelve or one o'clock that day. I
know that I put three nightdresses into one basket and
beside them Miss Elizabeth Kent made up her own bun-
dle for herself. Miss Constance came to the door of the
lumber-room after the things were in the basket, but I

<hr />

[1] On the occasion of Constance Kent's appearance before the magistrates on July 27, 1860. The evidence of Sarah Cox and Mrs. Holly is
quoted from Appendix II of *The Great Crime of 1860*.

have not quite finished packing them. She asked me if I would look in her slip pocket and see if she had left her purse there. I looked in the basket and told her it was not there. She then asked me to go down and get her a glass of water. I did so, and she followed me to the top of the back stairs as I went out of the room. I found her there when I returned with the water, and I think I was not gone near a minute, for I went very quickly. The lumber-room is on the same floor as the nursery. She drank the water and went up the other back stairs towards her own room. There was no further conversation between us. I covered down the basket and did not return to it. It was on Tuesday evening that I heard of the missing nightshirt, and I have never seen it since.

In cross-examination Sarah Cox amplified her statement:

On Saturday, June 30th, I took down a clean nightdress of Miss Constance's to be aired. I have heard that she had three altogether, but I did not know until after this. I took another clean nightdress to be aired on the following Saturday. Miss Constance's nightdresses are easily distinguishable from the other Misses Kents'. I never look over the clothes when they come from the wash. The dirty one put into the basket on the Monday after the murder, and the two I aired would make the three. I am clear that these were all Miss Constance's nightdresses. I did not observe any mark or stain upon the one that was put in the basket on the Monday, July 2nd. It appeared to have been dirtied as one would have been which had been nearly worn a week by Miss Constance.

The book in which the linen is entered is sent with

clothes to the washerwoman. The clothes were entered in the book on the Monday after the murder by Miss Kent. On the Monday next after that, July 9th, the clothes were not sent to the wash in the usual way. Mrs. Holly is the name of the washerwoman to whom the clothes were sent on the Monday after the murder. The washerwoman would not have the clothes on July 9th, because there was some dispute about the nightdress. I first heard that the nightdress was missing on the Tuesday evening after the murder. A message was sent from Mrs. Holly's daughter which I received from her. She said that there were three nightdresses put down on Mrs. Kent's book and only two sent, and her mother said that it was Miss Constance's that was missing and that I must send another as the policeman had been there that day to know if she had the same number of clothes sent that week as she always had, and that her mother had told him that she had. She said that her mother said that she must have another one sent, as she was afraid that the policeman was coming again and that if one was not sent, she must go to the policeman about it.

I told her that I was sure that she had made a mistake, as I was certain that I had put three nightdresses in the basket, and that I was quite sure one of those was Miss Constance's. The clothes, including the nightdress worn by Miss Constance during the week after the murder were not sent to the wash at all. On the following Saturday, I believe, Miss Constance borrowed a nightdress of her sister's, there being then the two dirty ones belonging to her in the house, which had been worn by her between June 30th and July 7th and 14th. I am certain that I put the nightdress of Miss Constance into the basket, but I can't swear that it went out of the house, as I was not in the house at the time.

Mrs. Holly, the laundress, then gave evidence.

> I recollect going for the clothes on the Monday after the murder. When I got to the house I saw the cook. We went upstairs to the spare room where the clothes were generally kept. The cook brought down one basket and I the other. I then secured the clothes in the basket and went out and called my daughter, Martha. The clothes were in the same state as I always receive them. Mrs. Kent's dress was on one basket and something else on the other. I and my daughter went straight home with the clothes. We heard that there was a nightdress missing and we opened the basket within five minutes after we got home and found that one was missing. It was not our usual custom to open the clothes so soon after receiving them. We heard a rumour that the nightdress was missing.

Where this rumour originated is something of a mystery. The police, as will be seen, did not visit Mrs. Holly until the Tuesday after the murder. Superintendent Foley of Trowbridge searched Road Hill House on the morning of Saturday, June 30th, and requested Dr. Parsons to assist him. The latter, in his evidence before the inquiry said:

> I accompanied Mr. Foley in searching the house and went into Miss Constance Kent's room. I examined the linen in her drawers and the nightcap and nightgown which were on the bed. They were all perfectly free from any stains of blood. The nightdress was very clean, but I cannot say how long it had been worn.

It seems possible that Dr. Parsons may have been indiscreet. Perhaps he talked about the cleanliness of the nightgown and the obvious inference to be drawn from this. The rumour which reached Mrs. Holly's ears can only be accounted for by some such inference.

Mrs. Holly said that she had not seen anything of the missing nightdress. Her house and her two daughters had been searched by the police for the dress without success.

I had the clothes home about twelve o'clock on the Monday following the murder, and in about five minutes after began to search for something that was missing. I did not say anything to the housemaid about anything being missing. I have three daughters. All three daughters were present when I examined the clothes that I brought from Mr. Kent's. I went up to get my money the next day between eleven and twelve o'clock and saw Mrs. Kent about the missing dress the same evening. I was told then that they were quite sure that Miss Constance's nightdress had been sent. The police came to my house the first time on the Tuesday evening. I am quite clear about it. Four constables came together and the parish constable as well. I was quite alarmed about it.

Mrs. Holly might well have been alarmed at such an invasion. But the police had not come to inquire about the nightdress, but to see whether Mrs. Holly could recognize the piece of flannel found with the body. Thus reassured, she decided to say nothing about the nightdress.

I knew the nightdress was missing at the time, but I did not say anything to them—the police—about it. I told them the clothes were all right by the book. They came to me about the nightdress on the next day. I was expecting the nightdress to be sent to satisfy the book, the same as the other clothes came sometimes.

No further evidence on this subject was adduced. It seemed to Whicher that quite enough had been said to show what had actually happened. The nightdress seen by Foley and Parsons on the morning after the murder was not the one which Constance had worn the previous night. It had been taken from her chest of drawers after the commission of the crime. This, after being worn on Saturday and Sunday night, was put into the washing basket. Having dispatched the housemaid for a glass of water Constance had abstracted it from the basket to make it appear that it had been lost in the wash. The nightdress in which she had actually committed the crime had been destroyed. She would thus have been found to be short of a nightdress and endeavour to account for this by making it appear that one had been lost in the wash.

The solicitor for the defence, however, contrived to push the evidence aside. He protested against the arrest of Constance on the grounds that "a paltry bedgown was missing". He then proceeded to a vicious attack upon Whicher:

And where is the evidence? The sole fact—and I am ashamed in this land of liberty and justice to refer to it—is the suspicion of Mr. Whicher, a man eager in pursuit of the murderer and anxious for the reward that has been offered. And it is upon his suspicion, unsupported by the slightest evidence whatever, that this step has been taken. The prosecution's own witnesses have cleared up the point about the bedgown, but because the washerwoman says that a certain bedgown was not sent to her, you are asked to jump to the conclusion that it was not carried away in the clothes basket.

But there can be no doubt in the mind of any person that the right number of bedgowns has been fully accounted for, and that this little peg upon which he seeks to hang this fearful crime has fallen to the ground. It rested on the evidence of the washerwoman only, and against that you have the testimony of several other witnesses. I do not wish to find fault with Mr. Whicher unnecessarily, but I think in the present instance, his professional eagerness in pursuit of the criminal has led him to take a most unprecedented course to prove a motive.[1]

Constance appears to have displayed very little concern about her arrest. Whicher's own statement[2] is evidence of her composure.

I have made an examination of the premises and I believe that the murder was committed by an inmate of the house. From many inquiries I have made and from information which I have received, I sent for Constance Kent on Monday last to her bedroom, having first previously examined her drawers and found a list of her linen, which I now produce, on which are enumerated among other articles of linen, three nightdresses as belonging to her.

I said to her, "Is this a list of your linen?" and she replied, "Yes." I then asked, "In whose handwriting is it?" and she answered, "It is in my own writing." I said, "Here are three nightdresses. Where are they?" She replied, "I have two. The other was lost in the wash a week after the murder." She then brought the two I now produce. I also saw a nightdress and a nightcap on her bed, and said to her, "Whose are these?" She re-

---

[1] *Somerset and Wilts Journal.*
[2] On the occasion of his arrest of Constance Kent on July 20, 1860.

plied, "They are my sister's." The nightdresses were only soiled by being worn.

This afternoon, I again proceeded to the house and sent for the prisoner in the sitting-room. I said to her: "I am a police officer, and I hold a warrant for your apprehension, charging you with the murder of your brother, Francis Saville Kent, which I will read to you." I then read the warrant to her and she commenced crying and said, "I am innocent," which she repeated several times. I then accompanied her to her bedroom where she put on her bonnet and mantle, after which I brought her to this place. She made no further remarks to me.

On the occasion of her examination before the magistrate, we are told that "at half-past eleven, Constance Emily Kent came in, walking with a faltering step, and going up to her father gave him a trembling kiss."

Constance gave evidence before the magistrates on October 3rd, when the charge against Elizabeth was heard. On that occasion she said:

On Friday, the 29th of June, I was at home. I had been at home for about a fortnight. I had previously been to school as a boarder at Beckington. The little boy who was murdered was at home also. I last saw him in the evening when he went to bed. He was a merry, good-tempered lad, fond of romping. I was accustomed to play with him often. I had played with him that day. He appeared to be fond of me, and I was fond of him. I went to bed at about half-past ten in a room on the second floor, in a room between that of my two sisters and the two maid-servants. I remember my sister Elizabeth coming into my room that night. I went to sleep soon after that. I was nearly asleep then. I next woke at about half-past six in the morning. I did not awake in the course of the night, and I heard nothing to disturb me. I got up at half-past six. I had some time after that heard of my brother being missing.

In reply to questions by the counsel for the prosecution Constance made the following statement:

On the night of the murder she had slept in her night-dress. She had slept in that nightdress since the previous Sunday or Monday. She usually wore the same night-dress for a week and changed it on Sunday or Monday. This was the same nightdress that she had worn on Monday, Tuesday, Wednesday, Thursday and Friday. On the Saturday she had slept in the same nightdress she had worn on the previous night. She was not certain whether she had put the clean nightdress on, on the Sunday or the Monday. She did not know what had become of the nightdress of hers which was said to be missing. She had heard the prisoner go to her sisters' door on Saturday morning to ask if they had the child with them or had taken it away. She was dressing at the time. She heard Elizabeth knock at the door, and went to her own door to listen to hear what it was. Her door was quite close to her sisters'. At that time she was nearly dressed.[1]

It is, perhaps, unnecessary to recount the circumstances under which Constance actually confessed. We are told that,

[1]Following Stapleton, *op. cit.* Appendix III, reproduced from the *Bristol Daily Post*.

she came under religious influence five years after the crime when, filled with deep sorrow and remorse, she told the clergyman of the case, that in order to free others of any suspicion cast on them it was her duty to make a public confession of her guilt. She was told she was right to obey her conscience and make any amends she could. Her life, if spared, could only be one long penance.[1]

Constance appeared before the Trowbridge Bench on April 26, 1865. A contemporary report says:[2]

She walked with a step which betrayed no emotion, but with downcast eyes and took her seat in the dock. Her conduct in the dock was at first marked by great composure. The past five years had wrought a considerable change in her appearance, she being taller and much more robust and womanly than when she was previously in this neighbourhood. Her deposition was as follows: "I wish to hand in of my own free will, a piece of paper with the following written on it in my own handwriting, 'I, Constance Emily Kent, alone and unaided, did, on the night of the 29th of June, 1860, murder at Road Hill House, Wiltshire, one Francis Saville Kent. Before the deed, no one knew my intentions, nor after of my guilt. No one assisted me in the crime, nor in my evasion of discovery.' "

In reply to the chairman she replied that she had nothing further to say. The examination was adjourned and resumed on May 4th. Further evidence was taken at the

---

[1] The Sydney document.
[2] *Somerset and Wilts Journal.*

conclusion of the proceedings, when Constance was asked
if she desired to say anything in answer to the charge she
shook her head and appeared as unmoved as during the
greater part of the day. Constance appeared at the Wiltshire Assizes at Salisbury on July 21st. The proceedings
were very brief. She pleaded guilty and declared that she
was well aware of what the plea involved. Her counsel,
Mr. Coleridge, stated that the prisoner wished to inform
the court that she alone was guilty of the murder and that
she wished to make her guilt known and atone for the
crime with the view of clearing the character of others of
any suspicion that might have been unjustly attached to
them. It afforded him pleasure to have the melancholy duty
of stating that there was no truth whatever in the report
that the prisoner was induced to perpetrate the crime because of the harsh treatment received at the hands of her
stepmother, for Miss Constance Kent had always received
the most uniform kindness from that lady, and on his honour he believed it to be true.

She was sentenced to death; but, some days later, the
sentence was commuted to one of penal servitude for life.

It was known that Constance had made a full confession
to a Dr. Charles Bucknill, who had examined her for the
purpose of ascertaining her mental condition, and to her
solicitor, Mr. Rodway, in Trowbridge. It was Constance's
desire that this confession should be made public, and at
the end of August Dr. Bucknill published the following
letter.[1]

   I am requested by Miss Constance Kent to commu-
nicate the following details of her crime which she has

---

[1]Circulated to the Press at the end of August 1865.

confessed to Mr. Rodway, her solicitor, and to myself, and which she now desires to be made public.

Constance Kent first gave an account of the circumstances of her crime to Mr. Rodway, and she afterwards acknowledged to me the correctness of that account when I recapitulated it to her. The explanation of her motive she gave to me when, with the permission of the Lord Chancellor, I examined her for the purpose of ascertaining whether there were any grounds for supposing that she was labouring under mental disease. Both Mr. Rodway and I are convinced of the truthfulness and good faith of what she has said to us.

Constance Kent says that the manner in which she committed her crime was as follows:

A few days before the murder she obtained possession of a razor from a green case in her father's wardrobe and secreted it. This was the sole instrument which she used. She also secreted a candle and matches by placing them in the corner of the closet in the garden where the murder was committed. On the night of the murder she undressed herself and went to bed because she expected that her sisters would visit her room. She lay awake watching till she thought the household were all asleep, and soon after midnight she left her bedroom and went downstairs and opened the drawing-room door and window shutters.

She then went to the nursery, withdrew the blanket from between the sheet and the counterpane and placed it on the side of the cot. She then took the child from his bed and carried him downstairs to the drawing-room. She had on her nightdress and in the drawing-room she put on her galoshes. Having the child in one arm she raised the drawing-room window with the other hand and went round the house and into the closet, the child being wrapped in the blanket and still sleeping, and while the child was in this position, she inflicted the wound in the throat. She says that she thought the blood would never come and the child was not killed, so she thrust the razor into its left side and put the body with the blanket round it into the vault. The light burnt out. The piece of flannel which she had with her was torn from an old flannel garment placed in the wastebag, and which she had taken some time before and sewed it to use for washing herself.

She went back into her bedroom, examined her dress and found only two spots of blood on it. These she washed out in the basin, and threw the water, which was but little discoloured, into the footpan in which she had washed her feet overnight. She took another of her nightdresses and got into bed. In the morning her nightdress had become dry where it had been washed. She folded it up and put it into the drawer. Her three nightdresses were examined by Mr. Foley, and she believes also by Dr. Parsons, the medical attendant of the family. She thought the bloodstains had been effectively washed out, but on holding the dress up to the light a day or two afterwards she found the stains were still visible. She secreted the dress, moving it from place to place, and eventually burned it in her own bedroom, and put the ashes or cinders into the kitchen grate. It was about five or six days after the child's death that she burnt the nightdress.

On the Saturday morning, she having cleaned the razor, she took an opportunity of replacing it unobserved in a case in the wardrobe. She abstracted the nightdress from the clothes-basket when the housemaid went to fetch a glass of water. The strange garment found in the boiler hole had no connexion whatever with these. As regards the motive of her crime, it seems that although she entertained at one time a great regard for the present Mrs. Kent, yet if any remark was at any time made which in her opinion was disparaging any member of the first family, she treasured it up and determined to revenge it. She had no ill-will against the little boy except that as one of the children of her stepmother. She declared that both her father and her stepmother had always been kind to her personally, and the following is a copy of the letter which she addressed to Mr. Rodway on this point while in prison before her trial:

DEVIZES, *May 15th*

Sir,—It has been stated that my feelings of revenge were excited in consequence of cruel treatment. This is entirely false. I have received the great kindness from both the persons accused of subjecting me to it. I have never had any ill-will towards either of them on account of their behaviour to me which has been very kind. I shall be obliged if you will make use of this statement in order that the public may be undeceived on this point.

I remain, Sir,

Yours most truly,

CONSTANCE E. KENT

She told me that when the nursemaid was accused she had fully made up her mind to confess if the nurse had been convicted, and that she had also made up her mind to commit suicide if she herself was detected. She said that she had felt herself under the influence of the devil before she committed the murder, but that she did not believe and had not believed that the devil had more to do with her crime than he had with any other wicked action. She had not said her prayers for a year before the murder and not afterwards till she came to reside at Brighton. She said that the circumstances which revived religious feelings in her mind was thinking about receiving sacrament when confirmed.

An opinion has been expressed that the peculiarities evinced by Constance Kent between the ages of twelve and seventeen may be attributed to the then transition period of her life. Moreover, the fact of her cutting off her hair and dressing herself in her brother's clothes and leaving home with the intention of going abroad, which occurred when she was only thirteen years of age, indicated a peculiarity of disposition and great determination of character which foreboded that, for good or evil, her future life would be remarkable.

This peculiar disposition which led to such singular violent resolves and actions, seems also to colour and intensify her thoughts and feelings and magnify into wrongs that were to be revenged, any little incidents or occurrences which provoked her displeasure.

Although it became my duty to advise her Counsel that she evinced no symptoms of insanity at the time of my examination, and that so far as it was possible to ascertain the state of her mind at so remote a period, there was no evidence of it at the time of the murder, I am yet of the opinion that, owing to the peculiarities of her constitution, it is probable that under prolonged solitary confinement she would become insane.

The validity of this opinion is of importance now that the sentence of death has been commuted to penal servitude for life, for no one should desire that the punishment of the criminal should be so carried out as to cause danger of a further and greater punishment not contemplated by the law.

This confession, which is undoubtedly authentic, is a most extraordinary document. The first question which arises is naturally that of motive. When he arrested Constance in 1860, Inspector Whicher realized the difficulty of proving an adequate motive for the murder. He hoped to establish this by calling a Miss Emma Moody, a school friend of Constance's. But Miss Moody's evidence was disappointing. The following is a sufficient extract:

I have heard her make such remarks about the child as this, that she disliked the child and pinched it, but I believe more from fun than anything else, for she was laughing at the time she said it. It was not this child more than the others. She said that she liked to tease them, this one and his younger brothers and sisters. I believe it was through jealousy and because the parents showed great partiality. I have remonstrated with her on what she said. I was walking with her one day towards Road, and I said, "Won't it be nice to go home for the holidays so soon." She said, "It may be to your home but mine's different." She also led me to infer, but I don't remember her precise words, that she did not dislike the child, but through the partiality shown by the parents the second family were much better treated than the first. I remember her saying that several times. We were talking about dress on some occasions and she said, "Mamma will not let me have anything I like, and if I said I would like a brown dress she would make me black, and the contrary." I remember no other conversation about the deceased child. She has only slightly referred to him.

This evidence was utterly inconclusive in supplying any motive for murder. Whicher was bitterly disappointed with

it. He said later:[1] "The witness, Miss Moody, in reference
to animus, did not give the evidence I was given to understand she could have done."

But there is no doubt that Constance's crime was directed, not against the victim, but against her stepmother.

She vowed she would avenge her mother's wrong, if
she devoted her life to it. After brooding over it for
some time, she resolved that as her stepmother had
robbed her mother of her father's love, she would de-
prive her of something she loved best. She then planned
and carried out her most brutal and callous crime, one
so vile and unnatural that people could not believe it
possible for a young girl.[2]

This last is probably as near the truth as it is possible
to get. Constance wished to be revenged on her stepmother, but not for any wrongs that she herself directly
suffered. Her immature mind had brooded upon the circumstances which she had observed during her childhood,
and these circumstances developed themselves into the
crime committed against her mother and the whole of the
family. Her eldest brother had chosen the sea as a profession, probably because a seafaring life appealed to him.
But Constance believed that he had done so merely to
escape from the intrusion of Miss Pratt into the family
circle. He had died abroad. To Constance this was a direct
result of having been driven from home. There is plenty
of evidence that the second family received preferential
treatment by their parents. In Constance's eyes this was
magnified into a martyrdom of the children of the first

[1] In his letter of November 23, 1860.
[2] The Sydney document.

Mrs. Kent. She believed that her younger brother, William, who shared her extraordinary escapade in 1876, was not to be given a fair chance in life. This may or may not have been true at the time. Certainly Mr. Kent evinced more interest in the prospects of his younger children. Finally, there was ever present in her mind a deep resentment at the position of authority achieved by a mere governess. She was old enough, at the time of the crime, to have formed the opinion that this position had been achieved by questionable means.

In her confession she insisted that she bore no ill-will towards her stepmother. This must be interpreted to mean that she bore no ill-will on account of any personal treatment which she had received from her. The clue to the motive appears to lie in another sentence of that confession.

> Although she entertained at one time a great regard for the present Mrs. Kent, yet if any remark was at any time made which in her opinion was disparaging to any member of the first family, she treasured it up and was determined to revenge it.

One may perhaps realize the cumulative effect of such a determination on a child of Constance's nature. She remembered every fancied slight. The second Mrs. Kent was not popular either with the neighbours or the servants. Constance must have heard a thousand suggestions that she was no better than she should be. Her final conclusions must have been that the household had been invaded by an immortal tyrant, who, owing to the influence she exercised over Mr. Kent, was secure from punishment. She felt this to be unjust. Punishment was deserved, and

could be inflicted were anyone bold enough to assume the
rôle of avenger.

Having decided that her stepmother must be punished,
Constance must have reflected upon the form which the
punishment should take. Punishment inflicted directly was
obviously beyond her powers. But Mrs. Kent was devoted
to her children, especially to the boy Francis. If anything
should happen to Francis Mrs. Kent would feel the blow
as acutely as though it had been directed at herself.

It does not seem to have occurred to Constance that the
blow would be almost as acutely felt by her father, to
whom she was apparently genuinely attached. Perhaps she
believed that her father would soon recover from his sorrow at the death of his youngest son. Mr. Kent had en-
dured such bereavements before without showing any signs
of being overwhelmed by them. At the date of the crime
he had already had thirteen children, and was expecting
the arrival of a fourteenth. Five of these had died in their
early infancy. Surely by this time such calamities must
have lost their power to depress him unduly!

Constance appears to have experimented with the possibility of making away with Francis. There is very little
doubt that she had determined upon the form which the
punishment of Mrs. Kent was to take some time before
1860. It so happened that, one night some two years before the crime, Mrs. Kent, Constance, and the two children of the second marriage were the only occupants of
the house besides the servants. Francis slept in the nursery
with the nurse. During the night the nursery must have
been entered, for in the morning Francis was found in his
cot with the bedclothes stripped off and his bed-socks
missing. It was never discovered how this happened. But
Constance was believed to have been at the bottom of it
and it was attributed to her well-known spirit of mischief.

It was possible that she believed that the exposure of the child would cause his death. It is remarkable that this incident was not mentioned during the inquiry into the cause of the crime.

It is an axiom of criminal investigation that every confession, whether genuine or not, is open to suspicion on the grounds of detail. The criminal may be willing to confess but not, for some strange psychological reason, to reveal his methods. Constance's confession appears to be no exception to this rule. It is almost incredible that she should have committed the crime by the method to which she confessed.

It is admitted that the methods of the local police in investigating the crime were elementary in the extreme. But the following facts are incontrovertible. Dr. Parsons, as soon as he saw the body, decided that the throat must have been cut with some sharp instrument. It is true that at the inquest he declared that the wound in the breast could not have been produced by a razor. But Dr. Parsons changed his opinion so frequently that too much reliance must not be placed upon his statement. In any case, on Saturday morning, the idea of a sharp instrument was firmly impressed upon his mind. And he succeeded in conveying this impression to Superintendent Foley.

Now Superintendent Foley, Dr. Parsons, and apparently dozens of others, searched the house from top to bottom early on Saturday morning. One may be allowed to presume that their search was directed primarily towards the discovery of a sharp instrument. Indeed, they made detailed inquiry into the knives cleaned by the garden boy that morning. But surely it must have occurred to them that there are other sharp instruments in the house. And of these sharp instruments, perhaps Mr. Kent's razors were the most obvious of all.

Yet Constance Kent in her confession says that a few days before the murder she obtained possession of a razor from a green case in her father's wardrobe and secreted it. This was the sole instrument she used. On the Saturday morning, having cleaned the razor, she took an opportunity of replacing it unobserved in the case in the wardrobe. This seems amazing. She abstracted the razor a few days before the murder. It is possible that Mr. Kent did not notice the absence of this particular razor. He may have put it aside for a time. But how could Constance tell that he would not discover that it had not been removed from its usual place? If he had done so, she could hardly have ventured to use it subsequently. And the difficulty of replacing the razor unobserved on the Saturday morning seems almost insuperable. It is true that Mr. Kent had left the house shortly after being informed of the disappearance of his son, but almost immediately afterwards the house was invaded by a band of searchers, and Constance, self-possessed though she undoubtedly was, would hardly have faced the risk of being accosted with a razor in her hand.

On the whole it seems that her statement regarding the razor was without foundation. She declared that the razor was the sole instrument with which she had done the deed. Dr. Parsons' opinion as to the possibility of the wound in the breast having been inflicted by a razor has already been quoted. It is unnecessary to examine the medical evidence at length. But the statement of Mr. Stapleton, who was present at the post-mortem and actually assisted in it, is worthy of attention. He says:

> Upon the left side of the body below and to the outer side of the nipple, a sharp blade had been passed diagonally over the fifth rib. Severing wholly the cartilage

of the sixth, partially that of the seventh rib, it had been thrust into the chest behind the membranous covering of the heart, which it had grazed without entering it. It then penetrated the diaphragm, and had grazed the stomach in a similar manner, without piercing the cavity. In its passage or during its withdrawal this blade had been violently twisted or wrenched round as was evident from the torn appearance of the muscular fibres, and the scraped irregular appearance of the exposed rib at the posterior angle of the cut and the appearance remarkably contrasted with the simple smooth surface of the other parts of its edges, and affording a reasonable inference that it was inflicted with a murderous intent and under some ferocious impulse. Very little blood had flowed from this stab, and none was found adherent to the side, nor was any coagulated upon the corresponding parts of the nightshirt. This stab injured no vital organ nor would it have caused immediate death. It would have been followed by very little bleeding, even if the heart's action and the circulation in its vessels were still going on at the time of its infliction. Its position and appearances afford no ground for the assumption that it was done by using the knife to thrust down the body of the child into the closet.[1]

Now it will be observed that though Mr. Stapleton does not expressly say that this wound could not have been inflicted with a razor, his language is very significant. He speaks repeatedly of a stab and of a knife. It is clearly impossible to inflict a stab with an ordinary razor, and the appearance of a wound inflicted by such a weapon is very different from that inflicted by a knife. It seems unlikely

---

[1] Stapleton, *op. cit.*

that Mr. Stapleton, who was a surgeon of considerable experience, should have spoken of a stab and a knife in describing a wound inflicted by a razor.

In many other details the confession seems difficult to believe. The mystery of the nightdress is certainly explained on the line of Whicher's theory. But may not this theory, already known to Constance, have inspired her account? She states in her confession that her three nightdresses were examined by Foley, and she believed also by Dr. Parsons, the medical attendant of the family. She thought the bloodstains had been effectively washed out, but on holding the dress up to the light a day or two afterwards, she found the stains were still visible. Now the whole object of the examination of the nightdress was to discover stains. Dr. Parsons, describing the incident before the Trowbridge magistrates, said:

I accompanied Mr. Foley in the search through the house, and in the course thereof went into Constance Kent's room. I examined her drawers and the night cap and the nightgown which were on the bed, and the whole of the bedding. The nightdress was perfectly free from any stains. The nightdress was very clean, but I could not speak as to whether it had on it the dirt resulting from a week's wear or not. There was nothing on Constance's nightdress which attracted my attention more than that it was very clean.

The attention paid to the nightdress lying on the bed, which was, of course, clean, may have distracted observation from the two found in the chest of drawers, but it seems incredible that though a medical man could find no bloodstains on either of the latter, they were visible to Constance a day or two afterwards. Again, Constance avers that, having found these tell-tale stains, she secreted the dress, moving it from place to place, and eventually burnt it in her own bedroom, and put the ashes of same into the kitchen grate. It was about five or six days after the child's death that she burnt the nightdress. The disappearance of a nightdress was apparently suspected from the first, since a rumour of it had reached Mrs. Holly's ears as early as the Saturday. Mrs. Holly herself confirms this disappearance. The local police were blunderingly though certainly actively looking for a nightdress. Yet Constance was able to move it about from place to place for five or six days and finally to burn it in her own bedroom. It hardly seems possible that she could have done this without arousing suspicion.

It must be admitted that queer things habitually happened at Road Hill House both before and after the murder. One of the queerest was revealed during the course of the Gilbertian inquiry held by Mr. Saunders on his own account. In the course of his examination of Police Constable Urch, the following extraordinary conversation[1] took place.

Were you present with Sergeant Watts in Road Hill House when he found a certain thing?—Yes; I was.

What was it?—Some woman's nightshift.

Where did Sergeant Watts find the article?—In the boiler hole.

Where was the boiler?—In the first kitchen going in, sir.

Was there anyone present? Was it at the entrance of the boiler hole or pushed far up?—It was in, sir, as if to light the fire.

[1]Quoted from Stapleton, *op. cit.* Appendix IV.

Was it dry or was it wet?—It was dry, sir, but very dirty.

What do you mean by dirty?—I mean as if it had been worn a long time.

What was the dirt upon it?—It had some blood about it.

Was it much blood or little? A large quantity or a small quantity?—There were several places with blood upon them.

Did they appear to have been there for some time?— Well, sir, I did not touch it myself. Sergeant Watts unfolded it, looked at it, and carried it to the coach-house.

Were there any initials on the shift?—I do not know, sir; I did not see any.

Was it a coarse article or a fine article of dress—such as servants wear or more like what young ladies wear?— I should think, sir, it was one of the servants.

Was it the size for a full-grown servant or a young woman—a full-grown woman servant or a nursegirl?— It was not a large one. We remarked two or three others there, but it was a small one.

It transpired that the shift had been given to Foley, who apparently suppressed it. He certainly never informed Whicher of the discovery. It may be urged with some truth that this is more incredible than anything in Constance's confession. A crime is committed under circumstances which make the discovery of a bloodstained nightdress indispensable. Something of the kind is actually found on the night after the murder. Yet a responsible officer of police is so satisfied that the shift could have no connexion with the crime that the existence of it is never mentioned. It is impossible to ignore the possibility that this blood-stained shift was actually the nightdress worn by Constance during the commission of the crime. How and when she conveyed it to the boiler hole is not apparent. But she may have done so immediately after returning to the house from the earth-closet. The evidence that either Foley or Dr. Parsons saw three nightdresses belonging to her on Saturday morning is not conclusive. Constance, in her confession, denies that the shift had any connexion with the deed. But, as has already been pointed out, too much reliance must not be placed upon the details of this confession.

The route taken by her when carrying the child from the nursery to the earth-closet has been questioned. And yet, in this particular, the confession is probably correct. It was certainly not the shortest route she could have taken, but any alternative route had its disadvantages. The most obvious way to reach the earth-closet from the house was to leave the house by the back door and cross the yard. But the watchdog was at large in the yard. He might have barked and raised the alarm. Actually there is evidence of a kind that the dog did bark that night. An anonymous policeman is said to have declared that about one o'clock on the night of the murder, the house dog barked as he passed the house. Again:

> Two men, one of them named Joe Moon, were on the night of the murder working in a neighbouring quarry or limekiln. Very early in the morning they heard the house dog barking loudly, and remarked one to the other, "There must be something wrong at Mr. Kent's. The dog is barking so."[1]

Constance may therefore have actually passed through the yard. The next most direct route would be through the

[1] From an article in the *Somerset and Wilts Journal.*

front door, and so to the earth-closet, without passing
through the yard at all. Why the window of the drawing-
room should have been taken as the means of exit from
the house it is difficult to say. This window was situated
at almost the farthest point of the house from the closet,
and its use involved a journey round two sides of the
house and, incidentally, a passage under the windows of
the room in which Mr. and Mrs. Kent were sleeping. It
was, in fact, the most roundabout route which could have
been chosen.

So much for the confession and for the very curious
problems to which it gives rise. But it must not be forgotten that the evidence of Constance's guilt rests entirely
upon this confession. Her trial at the Assizes took no more
than a few minutes. She pleaded guilty and her counsel
then made a short statement. This concluded the proceedings, and the judge sentenced her to death. Very general
regret was expressed at the time that no trial had taken
place. Had Constance pleaded not guilty, much that remains unexplained might have been revealed. It was said
at the time,[1] apparently with authority, that thirty-five witnesses would have been called, and that their united statements would have presented the case against the prisoner
in a manner which would have left no reasonable doubt of
her guilt quite irrespective of her confession. The point is,
that these thirty-five witnesses must have been available in
1860. It is extremely improbable that they could have given
any fresh evidence five years after the crime had been
committed.

The temptation to speculate as to what would have happened had not the investigations into the crime been so
hopelessly bungled is almost irresistible. The proceedings

[1] In an article in the *Daily Telegraph*.

at the inquest were farcical. The one aim of the coroner and of the foreman of the jury seems to have been to exonerate the members of the family. They could not believe that persons of their station in life could have committed such a crime. Much the same reluctance even to consider their guilt seems to have inspired the local police. They acted from the first upon this theory. No member of the family could possibly have committed the crime. Therefore the criminal must be sought among the servants, or some intruder from outside must be imagined.

Inspector Whicher was the first to tackle the case scientifically. That he failed to establish his case is by no means to his discredit. It must be remembered that he did not arrive on the scene until a fortnight after the crime, by which time several important clues had undoubtedly been destroyed. He was also an object of local jealousy. Nobody concerned, from Superintendent Foley to the parish constable, had the slightest intention of allowing a stranger to succeed where they had failed if they could possibly help it. They withheld information from him, and there is reason to suppose that they even deliberately misled him. Scotland Yard was in those days a comparatively recent institution and had not yet gained the confidence either of the county constabularies or of the public.

A leading authority upon criminal investigation[1] has said:

> The scene of the crime must be inspected both in its general aspect and in detail, and must be considered as far as possible in relation to the facts. The time allotted to this close examination is far from being lost and the

[1] Dr. Hans Gross, *Criminal Investigation*, London, Sweet and Maxwell.

results compensate largely for the apparent delay. After this, the investigating officer must find out the persons best able to give information about the case, which will enable him to become at least approximately acquainted with the circumstances. Habit, above all, helps the investigating officer in examining people with a view to obtaining this preliminary information. He learns little by little not to waste time over details, while forgetting nothing of importance.

Had Whicher been summoned, and had he arrived on the scene on Saturday following the crime, would he have been able to reach success upon these lines?

He would, at all events, have been confronted with a mass of conflicting evidence. Even the medical evidence was apparently unreliable. At the time of the inquest Dr. Parsons stated that he was of the opinion that death had not been due to suffocation, that the child had not been even partially suffocated at the time the fatal wound was inflicted. This opinion was upheld both by Mr. Stapleton and by the coroner, himself a surgeon. By 1865, however, Mr. Stapleton had changed his mind. In the course of his evidence before the Trowbridge Bench, he said:

> In my opinion, the incision in the throat was the immediate cause of death, but the appearance of the place where the body was found was such as to induce me to suppose that the throat was not cut there, or that the circulation of the child was in a great degree stopped by suffocation before it was done.

Any sort of attempt to establish motive would have been hopeless. We have already seen how Miss Moody's evidence disappointed Whicher's expectations. Had Mr. Stapleton in his capacity as friend of the family been consulted, his statement would have been verbose and unsatisfactory.

As she grew up, Constance manifested a strong, obstinate, and determined will, and her conduct, even as a little child, gave evidences of an irritable and impassioned nature. Whether the governess possessed that experience and tact and moral weight which fitted her for the responsible and arduous duties she had undertaken, whether in the delicate and unusual position in which she consented to remain in Mr. Kent's family, she taught her heart to lavish on that child the unceasing and considerate care, and motherly tenderness and patience, which its more than orphanage required, these are questions to which her memory and conscience only can reply. It is not expressed or intimated by those who observed her conduct, and must have watched and criticized it too, that she was either unfaithful or unequal to this difficult and trying task. . . . That Constance was ever treated with cruelty by her stepmother is emphatically denied even by her own sisters. Amongst our social evils, troublesome children and indiscreet, impatient parents are not uncommon, nor are they incurable, and these details can assume importance in this family only in consequence of the events which have since transpired and which have originated the presumption, perhaps neither correct nor warrantable, of the child's irritation and dislike of a relation which had been imposed upon it, and against which other resistance was impossible.[1]

[1]Stapleton, *op. cit.*

Whicher would have immediately arrived at the conclusion that some person sleeping in the house on that night had committed the crime. Had he been called to the scene at once he would have been able to interview all these people before their minds had become distracted by a flood of rumour and gossip. He would have inquired into the history and habits of each of them, and would very soon have come to the conclusion that Constance was an abnormal child. The motive of the crime, though inexplicable to the normal mind, would then have transpired.

Whicher would probably have been able to elucidate the exact truth about the nightdresses. Had it been Whicher, instead of Foley and Parsons, who examined the house on the Saturday morning, the very obvious clues which then existed would not have escaped his attention. He would not have mistaken a roughly washed and dried nightdress for a clean one. And he most certainly would not have rested until he had satisfied himself about all the sharp weapons to be found in the house. Whether or not he would have succeeded in breaking down the resistance of the one person who must have guessed the secret from the first is very doubtful. It is impossible to believe that Mr. Kent can have had any doubts as to the identity of the culprit. He was aware of the peculiarity of Constance's nature, and he had plenty of experience of her erratic behaviour. By a process of elimination alone he must have come to the conviction of his daughter's guilt. By his silence, he placed himself in a terrible position. From the date of the crime until Constance's confession, he was very widely suspected of having been guilty of the murder of his son. He found himself between the horns of an awful dilemma. He must either endure the obloquy to which a suspected murderer is subject, or he must divulge his own suspicions, and so bring about the arrest, and most probably the conviction, of his daughter.

It may perhaps be permissible as to Constance's character. Of her appearance there is no reliable record. We are told that "no likeness or description of Constance is accurate." She always, as much as possible, concealed her features and slipped out of sight if strangers came near. In a contemporary report of her appearance at the Assizes, it is stated that "she is an exceedingly plain-looking young person, and totally unlike the photographs which are sold as portraits of her. She has a broad, full and uninteresting face which wears more an expression of stupid dullness than intelligence." We can only suppose that her expression on this occasion belied her. Stupid dullness is certainly not a characteristic of her crime and of her subsequent conduct. She contrived, in spite of Whicher's suspicions, to create an impression of her innocence and to secure public sympathy. On the other hand, her undoubted intelligence is not that associated with the criminal type. Constance was not by any means a born criminal. Her crime was not committed upon personal grounds. No doubt, she had by slow degrees convinced herself that she was the individual appointed by Providence as the avenger of wrongs. She wished to punish her stepmother and she certainly hit upon the most effective means of doing so. It will be argued that she showed disregard of human life and that therefore she must have had criminal instincts. But it is more probable that she believed that she was offering a sacrifice rather than committing a murder. A sacrifice to her mother's memory and for the fancied wrongs of her children. Abraham would have sacrificed his son in the interests of his own welfare had not the angel of the Lord restrained him. No such divine interference manifested itself in favour of Constance's victim. She may

have interpreted this as a sign of approval on the part of
Providence at whose behest she believed herself to be acting. It is probable that she never gave a thought to the
consequences which must inevitably follow her deed. She
probably believed that the murderer of the child would
remain undiscovered and that the deed itself would soon
be forgotten. She could not have anticipated the storm of
abuse and suspicion which would burst on the whole family.

She seems to have foreseen that such a callous and brutal murder would not be attributed to a girl of sixteen. She
was undoubtedly sufficiently intelligent to count upon this.
Contrition she certainly never felt until she eventually confessed under the influence of religious emotion. And, even
then, the whole of her confession seems to suggest the
absence of true contrition. She confessed, not to save her
own soul, but to remove the load of suspicion from others.
It is possible that the original idea of justification never
left her till very much later.

It is possible that, in a sense, the crime saved her character. Before it there is ample evidence that she was a
wayward, passionate girl. She showed little or no consideration for others and she would probably have developed
into a selfish, headstrong woman. After the crime, her
character seems to have changed entirely.

It was obviously impossible for the Kent family to remain at Road Hill House. They went for a short time to
Weston-super-Mare, but found themselves still too near
the scene of the tragedy. From Weston-super-Mare, they
removed to Wales, but Constance did not accompany them.
This is surely evidence that Mr. Kent at least was fully
cognisant of the secret. Constance left England and stayed
for a couple of years at a convent in France. Not, to be
noted, as an inmate, but as a pupil. In 1863 she came back

to England, where she stayed as a visitor in a religious
house at Brighton. From all that can be gleaned of her life
during this period, it was seen that this seclusion was in
accordance with her own wishes. Her rebellious nature
seems to have entirely changed and to have been replaced
by an intense desire to live under some sort of discipline.
We may conjecture that the latter was an illustration of her
true nature. Her turbulent childhood may have been merely
the reaction to Mrs. Kent's injudicious treatment.

After her reprieve Constance remained in prison until
1885. Various glimpses of her during that period remain,
but unfortunately most of them are mutually contradictory.
A single instance will serve to show how contradictory are
these glimpses. Major Arthur Griffiths, in *Secret of the
Prison House*, says:

> Constance Kent, whom I remember at Millbank, was
> first employed in the laundry and afterwards as a nurse
> in the Infirmary. A small, mouse-like little creature,
> with much of the promptitude of the mouse or the liz-
> ard's surprise in disappearing when alarmed. The ap-
> proach of any strange or unknown face whom she feared
> might come to spy her out and stare, constituted a real
> alarm for Constance Kent. No doubt there were features
> in her face which the criminal anthropologist would have
> seized as suggesting an instinctive criminality. High
> cheek-bones, a lowering overhanging brow and deep-
> set small eyes. But yet her manner was prepossessing
> and her intelligence was of a high order.

A correspondent who acted for a time as chaplain of
Fulham Convict Prison, informed the author that he remembers Constance being confined there. It was his duty
to visit her and read her letters at a time when she was

pleading for her release. He also says that he does not at
all agree with Major Griffiths' description of her. On the
other hand, we are told[1] that Major Griffiths' description
of her is about nearest to the truth. Her best points were
a fresh complexion and a quantity of golden brown hair.
On one point all accounts of her prison life are, however,
agreed. She was docile and uncomplaining. She was for a
time confined in Portland Prison, where she executed a
series of mosaics. These are still be to seen in the Chapel
of St. Peter's and have been much admired.

After her release she disappeared from view. The legend
that she married a clergyman is entirely without foundation, as are many of the legends connected with her and
with her family. The anonymous correspondent so frequently quoted, says: "After her release she changed her
name and went overseas and, single-handed, fought her
way to a good position, and made a home for herself,
where she was well-liked and respected before she died."

Constance remains, in spite of all research, an elusive
personality. That she escaped detection is probably her
greatest claim to fame. But the science of detection was
then in its infancy, and local prejudice was in her favour.
Mr. and Mrs. Kent had for long been unpopular with their
neighbours. The crime, it was argued, could not have been
committed by a mere girl, and it was unlikely that it had
been committed by Mrs. Kent. Mr. Kent's unpopularity
made of him a scapegoat welcome to local opinion. Who
but a strong and determined man could have committed
such a crime? The motives attributed to him are too scan-
dalous to be worthy of repetition. Whicher probably made
insufficient allowance for local prejudice and acted too
hastily. The evidence which he was able to produce was

[1]The Sydney document.

inconclusive. He did not hope for an immediate conviction of Constance, but for a remand. He was of the opinion that had she remained in custody she would have confessed. This opinion was possibly optimistic. Constance knew that public sympathy was on her side. Unless Whicher had been able to obtain conclusive evidence in the matter of the nightdresses, unless he had been able to produce the weapon with which the crime was committed, Constance would probably have remained obdurate. And in that case, as she knew well enough, her release could only be a matter of time. She had already shown that she possessed sufficient obstinacy and firmness of will to put up with any amount of temporary inconvenience.

But the remand was not granted and Whicher had to admit failure. Her counsel's speech on her behalf was frankly an appeal to sentiment. He adopted a tone of virtuous indignation. There was not a tittle of evidence against her, not one word on which the finger of infamy could be pointed against her. Although a most atrocious murder had been committed, it had been followed by a judicious murder no less atrocious. If the murderer were never discovered, it would never be forgotten that this young lady had been dragged like a common felon to Devizes Gaol. The fact alone was quite sufficient to ensure the sympathy of every man in the country and the kingdom. The steps which had been taken must blast her hopes and prospects for life. He besought the magistrates immediately to liberate the young lady and to restore her to her friends and her home.

The fact that this speech was greeted with applause is indicative of the difficulties with which Whicher had to contend.

But though Whicher failed, the reasons for his failure have already been pointed out. The Road Hill murder teaches a lesson which even in these days is apt to be overlooked. It is essential that, immediately after the discovery of a crime, the services of an experienced investigating officer should be secured. Where the scene of the crime is a large town, there is usually no difficulty about this. But in country districts the local police, however efficient they may be, have not as a rule the necessary experience. In spite of this they are sometimes loth to enlist the aid of Scotland Yard. The perils of such a course are accurately exemplified in the case of Constance Kent.

PART III

The Case of Adelaide Bartlett

by Margaret Cole

THIS is the story of Adelaide Bartlett, who stood her trial in the winter of 1885–6 for the death of her husband, Edwin Bartlett, after the coroner's inquest had resulted in a verdict of wilful murder. At the trial she had been acquitted, though the Judge's summing-up was distinctly unfavourable, and if a verdict of Not Proven had been possible under the English Law, that is the verdict that would have been given. When the verdict was announced there was "immense cheering" in court, which caused Mr. Justice Wills to exclaim: "This conduct is an outrage." One may, however, perhaps conclude that the British public, or some section of it, thought at the time that she ought not to have been hanged.

This trial is, I think, one of the most interesting of British criminal trials, first, because the tale is not a tale of horror or brutality. None of the people concerned, however odd, or, if you like, however foolish they may have been, were monsters; they were not even trying to be unkind to one another. Indeed, it would rather appear that they were all trying to be as nice as possible under rather difficult circumstances. No one ever heard the Bartletts disagree, and the first angry word was spoken after Edwin's death, when that somewhat feeble creature, the Reverend George Dyson, was endeavouring to ensure his own escape. The second reason is that it shows up the law's limitations in certain quite definite ways. It is very clear that, if you are going to get into trouble with the law, it does not pay to be odd, particularly if your oddity is in any way connected with your sexual or matrimonial relations.

Edwin Bartlett was undoubtedly an odd man, with uncommon (though by no means unheard-of) ideas on a good many subjects; and Adelaide Bartlett, his wife, who was much less odd, was very nearly hanged because in the year 1885 she had in her possession a book which discussed birth-control, and, what was more, had actually lent it to a gentleman friend.

Said the Judge: "Gentlemen, I cannot—sitting here—I cannot have such garbage passed under my eyes, and then allow it to go forth that an English judge concurs in the view that it is a specimen of pure and healthy literature." Ugh! Ugh! Ugh! Later, in his summing-up, his horror—the horror of the law at anything at all unusual, anything out of its ken—led him into the definite but not uncommon injustice of denying that the oddity existed at all. Said he: "It looks . . . as though we had two persons to deal with abundantly vulgar and commonplace in their habits and ways of life." But nobody who has read the evidence—and presumably the learned Judge had at least listened to it—can have any doubt that whatever Edwin Bartlett was, he was not commonplace. The Judge's remark was just a piece of gross prejudice, and if the prosecution could have suggested any really plausible way in which Adelaide Bartlett could have got a large quantity of chloroform into her husband's stomach, it would probably have succeeded in hanging her.

The trial also shows the curious and innate inability of the law to distinguish between types of untrue statement. The law assumes that people in giving evidence either speak the truth or tell lies, and further, that speaking the truth is quite easy. Either you do or you don't, and there's an end of it. It follows, first, that if two or more people lie confidently and cannot be proved to be lying, the law is more likely to accept their statements than those of one person whose evidence cannot be corroborated; and, secondly, that if a witness finds the truth difficult to explain, as every practical person knows that it very often is, and hesitates, qualifies, and appears to contradict himself, the law is very ready to brand that person as a liar, or, at the least, as "a very unsatisfactory witness". In this story, the unfortunate Dr. Leach, who seems to have been really doing his best to explain the curious circumstances of the Bartlett household, was heavily bullied by counsel and sat upon by the Judge at every turn. This sort of nursery mentality: "Now, Tommy, you can just give me a plain answer, yes or no, without any of your naughty quibbling. Did you and Harry spill that ink, or did you not?" "Well, nurse, you see, we didn't exactly *spill* it—" "None of your 'didn't exactlys'—into the corner with you!"—this sort of thing makes one wonder at times whether there is any real connexion between law and justice.

Finally, the law is even behind the nursery in that it does not appear to know, what every intelligent nurse or mother knows, that there is an enormous difference between lying in the strict sense and telling fairy-stories, between saying, "No, I did *not* take the plums," when you did, and saying, "Mother, I saw a whale in the pond this morning," or even, "Mother, I stayed awake for hours and hours last night." Everybody of any experience knows that there are many people who remain for the whole of their lives so much under the influence of their own emotional states that they are quite incapable of distinguishing between objective and subjective truth, so that their statements at different times flatly and perplexingly contradict one another. They are not lying in any sense that they would recognize to be lying; it is simply that their impression of what is happening or has happened has changed without their knowing it. And it is again clear, to any person of experience reading the Bartlett case, that there was a great deal of 'subjective evidence' about, which was given upon oath and believed by the witnesses, but which might or might not correspond to the facts. But the court, being the law, was unable to recognize this subjective evidence for what it was. It had either to accept it and make the best sense it could of the result, or, if it discovered that at some point it conflicted with some known fact, to call the witness a liar. For instance, Adelaide Bartlett told Dr. Leach that she was married at sixteen. She was not; she was nearly twenty. Therefore Adelaide Bartlett was a liar. But surely it was clear that she was not lying; she felt as though she had been married at sixteen, and, as the story went, she really might have been. That is not the way in which to get at the truth of facts which depend so largely on states of emotion.

But it is time to turn to the facts themselves, as they were brought out in court. It is necessary to be like Dr. Leach, and to add this qualification, because there are certainly many gaps missing which must be filled by conjec-

ture. In particular, we have to do without the voice of
Edwin Bartlett, who was in fact the centre of the picture.
It is very unfortunate that Edwin did not keep a diary. He
was exactly the sort of man who ought to have kept a
diary, and if he had, how useful it would have been!

The story begins, then, with Edwin Bartlett, grocer,
marrying Adelaide de la Tremouille, spinster, aged 19, in
1875. Adelaide came from Orléans; nothing is known
about her parentage, though it has been suggested that she
was illegitimate and had English blood. Edwin possessed
a father and at least two brothers, and a grocery business
in Herne Hill, which was about to become mildly prosperous; at least, at the time of his death, ten years later,
he and his partner were the owners of half a dozen grocers' shops.

Nothing, again, is known of Edwin's courtship; but almost immediately two unusual features appear. For his
first act after marriage was to send his nineteen-year-old
wife to school for a couple of years; it was not until 1877
that she came to live with him. Why he did this we do not
know; presumably he wanted her to be better educated,
as he seems to have been a man who had a great admiration for the sort of cheap learning that can be easily displayed. There have been other and more distinguished men
who set seriously about the business of educating their
wives, notably the estimable Thomas Day; but few of them
began so late in the subject's life.

Anyhow, in 1877, Adelaide, now, we trust, sufficiently
educated, came to Herne Hill and began to live with her
husband. It should be mentioned that her dowry, whatever
it was, seems to have been usefully employed in her husband's business; it is less clear to what purpose, if any,
her education was utilized. According to herself, she was
exhibited at intervals to entertain her husband's business

friends—for some time she had no friends at all of her own.

The Bartletts were, to all appearances, happy. But almost directly Edwin's mother died and his father came to live with them at Herne Hill. Old Mr. Bartlett, who was by now almost entirely dependent on his son, was undoubtedly a nasty old gentleman. He disliked and quarrelled with his daughter-in-law from the first; when Edwin fell ill he immediately suggested there was something wrong about it; when Edwin died he was prompt to indicate that his wife must have murdered him; and when he was put in the witness-box he did his best to blacken Adelaide's character, though he was a trifle hampered by the existence of a document, signed by himself some years previously, which decleared that all the accusations he had made were false. Edwin now being dead, he naturally stated that the document was signed under duress, and that every word he had said was true; but that was the sort of lie with which the law is capable of dealing.

The only fact of any importance which emerged from all this was that in 1878 or 1879 Adelaide ran away for a time. Nobody really knows where she ran to, or why; the most obvious probability is that she was 'fed up' with her father-in-law and possibly a bit bored.

In 1881 Adelaide was confined. The labour was very difficult and the child was stillborn. Edwin, who appears not to have liked doctors much until he was ill himself, would not have a doctor called until it was too late; and, whether or not Adelaide could have had another child, they did not make the experiment. The nurse who attended her was called Annie Walker. She seems to have been a pleasant and intelligent woman, and Adelaide, who it will be remembered, had at that time no woman friend, confided in her to some extent. But, as far as Annie Walker's recollections went, the confidences did not amount to much. Mrs. Bartlett said "her husband did not appreciate her work, and she worked beautifully." I should think most midwives have in their time listened to hundreds of similar confidences.

In 1881, also, Edwin fell ill. This is a very interesting fact, and I could wish that more information was available about it. He is said to have had a nervous breakdown, caused by laying a floor which is surely a very odd cause for a nervous breakdown. One could understand it better if he had strained his back or burst a blood-vessel; but no, he only had a nervous breakdown, necessitating a sea-voyage, and one is well enough acquainted with a certain type of mind to wonder whether it was not Adelaide's illness rather than the floor-laying which made Edwin feel that he must be ill himself and so secure a little sympathy and attention. However, this possibility interested nobody at the time, so we must leave it at that.

Thereafter the story proceeds uneventfully until the year of Edwin's illness and death. The Bartletts moved twice, becoming, one presumes, a little bit better off as time went on. They made acquaintance, at some time or other, with a couple called Matthews, who remained the only friends they had—though there is no evidence to show that they were ever really intimate. During the years between 1881 and 1885 Edwin, it would seem, got more and more wrapped up in his work, or, at any rate, said he did. "It was work, work, work with him all the time," old Mr. Bartlett exclaimed petulantly; and when, at some time in the latter year the Bartletts took a holiday at Dover, Edwin used frequently to catch a train at 3 a.m. in order to get up to business in town, where he sometimes stayed until eight in the evening. That in itself, one would think, would be more liable to lead to a nervous breakdown than any amount of floor-laying. However, in the meantime, he had found, or thought he had, a sufficient means of keeping his young wife from fretting.

For in the early months of 1885 the Bartletts had made the acquaintance of the Reverend George Dyson, who was then a Wesleyan minister at Putney. He was comparatively young, only 27 at the date of the trial, and from the first both the Bartletts were all over him. The principal reason for this seems to have been that he was better educated even than Adelaide after her husband had done all he could for her, and, furthermore, if one can say so without being unduly offensive, that his cultural goods were all in the shop window. There is not a particle of evidence that the Reverend George Dyson was really a person of deep or wide attainment. The poem which he wrote to Adelaide, and went to almost indecent lengths to recover, has for its final verse:

> Who is it that hath burst the door,
> Enclosed the heart that shut before,
> And set her queen-like on its throne,
> And made its homage all her own?
>   My Birdie——

and there is no reason to suppose that the rest of the poem was any better. On literary grounds, if no other, it was possibly wise to suppress it. But to say this is not to deny in the least that George Dyson may have been of great value, at any rate in the opening stages of their acquaintance, to the Bartlett pair. Everyone is perfectly familiar with the phenomenon of the person with a small amount of culture acting as guide, philosopher and friend to those who have less (much like last term's new boy smoothing the path of this term's new boy), and it is priggish to deny its value.

At any rate, Edwin Bartlett had no doubts at all. He jumped at George Dyson as a means of keeping Adelaide happy and occupied while he was away on business. Nor does that fact, fortunately for Adelaide, rest upon the evidence of either herself or George Dyson alone. From the attitude which both the prosecution and the Judge took up, it seems pretty clear that without inside confirmation they would have dismissed such a story, having already caught out both Dyson and Adelaide in misstatements of fact; but there was a letter in existence in Edwin's own handwriting which put the matter beyond all doubt. Here is the letter. It was written in September 1885, while the Bartletts were staying at Dover.

14 St. James Street,
Dover.
Monday.

Dear George,

Permit me to say I feel great pleasure in thus addressing you for the first time. To me it is a privilege that I am allowed to feel towards you as a brother, and I hope our friendship may ripen as time goes on, without anything to mar its brightness. Would that I could find words to express my thankfulness to you for the very loving letter you sent to Adelaide to-day. It would have done anybody good to see her overflowing with joy as she read it whilst walking along the street, and afterwards as she read it to me. I felt my heart going out to you. I long to tell you how proud I feel at the thought I would soon be able to clasp the hand of the man who from his heart could pen such noble thoughts. Who can help loving him? I felt that I must say two words, 'Thank

you', and my desire to do so is my excuse for troubling
you with this. Looking towards the future with joyful-
ness, I am,

Yours affectionately,
EDWIN.

Now it is quite idle to pretend, as the learned Judge
tried to pretend in his summing-up, having by then, as we
observed, decided that he was dealing only with "vulgar
commonplace people", that there is nothing remarkable
in this letter "beyond a little tendency towards over-
sentimentality". The over-sentimentality is there all right;
some might even suggest that what Edwin Bartlett did to
his new friend in the ministry was to slobber over him.
But it is certainly not the letter of what the law considers
an ordinary man. Ordinary men, the ordinary men whom
the law knows and whom the members of the jury are
considered to resemble, do not feel thankful to see their
wives overflowing with joy as they read other men's letters; they are more apt to scowl and frown. But Edwin
Bartlett overflowed with joy, and when he was absent encouraged the Reverend George Dyson to spend a considerable amount of time with Adelaide. While they lived at
Merton Dyson came nearly every day to see her, often
staying on after Edwin had returned from business. When
they were on holiday at Dover he ran down more than once
to call on them, and when they moved to Pimlico Edwin
presented him with a season ticket in order to facilitate his
visits, since the young Wesleyan minister, like most other
young Wesleyan ministers, had very little money of his
own. In fact, without taking into account the evidence of
anyone whose credibility in the eyes of the law was doubtful, it may safely be said that Edwin Bartlett shoved his
wife, if not exactly into the arms, at least into terms of

affectionate friendship with George Dyson. It must be observed also, however, that he did not shove her, nor did she enter upon anything which in police-courts would be called 'intimacy'. If there had been any evidence at all to show that George Dyson was Adelaide's lover in a police-court sense, we may be certain that the prosecution would have dragged it out. The best that they could find was that Dyson had kissed her, both in and out of her husband's presence, that she had been sitting on the floor with her head against his knee, and that upon one occasion the long lace curtains, which in the best Victorian fashion covered the sitting-room windows, were noticed by a servant to be pinned together. As, however, the door was not locked upon that or any other occasion, it cannot be supposed that there was any great attempt at concealment.

Finally, Edwin, as far as we know, continued to love and trust both the other members of the triangle until the end of his days. We must, of course, in fairness remember that, as I said earlier, we have not access to Edwin's private thoughts; but at least he uttered no derogatory word to anyone else. And in September 1885 he went off to his place of business and there altered his will, leaving Adelaide free to marry again without losing his money, and naming Dyson his executor. This does not prove, as Adelaide at one time suggested, that Edwin was contemplating his own speedy death; but it does surely show that he was contemplating that the close connexion between Dyson and his wife should continue whatever happened to him; and he can hardly have failed to think of the possibility that if he died the other two might marry.

Here, then, you have these three people, in October and November 1885, living on what were undoubtedly queer terms. They would be queer terms nowadays; they were

queerer in 1885, though it should be remembered that oddity is not an invention of the post-War period, nor confined
to the intelligentsia. Possibly grocers ought not to presume
to have curious views on society; but sometimes they have.

Anyhow, these three oddities seem to have been happy
enough, and for the moment we might take a look at them
and their characters before things went wrong. We know
least of Edwin, because he never appears before us in person; but we can get an idea of him—a man of forty, very
much devoted to work, with hardly any outside recreations
and no friends other than business acquaintances, except
George Dyson: a dutiful son, to the extent that he kept his
unpleasant old father and saw to it that he did not want,
but not so dutiful as to support him against his wife: and
undoubtedly an earnest and affectionate, if not a very
amusing or sensitive husband. He does not, as I have said,
seem to have any outside amusements to speak of; but he
had some intellectual interests, and liked to discuss, both
with George Dyson and with others, questions such as
mesmerism and the relations of the sexes.

Old Mr. Bartlett, who would have cut his tongue out
sooner than invent anything favourable to Adelaide, rec-
ollected him saying that a man ought to have two wives,
one to take out and one to do the work, and Dr. Leach
and George Dyson both deposed to curious conversations
they had with him. He told Dr. Leach at one time that he
was being mesmerized by a friend from a distance, and
with Dyson he discussed whether polygamy was permitted
by the Bible. Both Dyson and Leach, who were the only
men with whom he was on terms of intimacy, were much
impressed, in a way which they found difficult to explain
to the Judge, who continually and peevishly called for
'facts', with the abnormality of Edwin's views on matters
which were not matters of business; and the doctor went

so far as to wonder whether his patient was not suffering from delusions. Dr. Leach, it should be emphasized, was quite new to the situation, for he was only called in at the time of Edwin's last illness. It would seem as though Edwin had a mind that was interested in unorthodox ideas, but lacked both the educational training or the natural common sense that would have enabled him to judge among them. There are plenty of people of this type in the world; they are apt to be found among the ardent supporters of new religions, 'new' political parties and 'new' economics. Edwin, however, spent too much time on his business to be able to do more than talk about his views in private.

George Dyson's character came out quite clearly at the inquest and trial—much more clearly than he could at all have relished. He was a weak, sloppy-minded young fellow with a certain amount of looks, manners, and cheap culture, whose head had been turned by the admiration of those two who were his seniors. It may well be that this was the first occasion upon which such admiration had come his way, for he was not, according to the *Daily Telegraph*, a very good preacher; and if he had been passionately devoted to his own calling it is strange that he was able to give up so much time to educating Adelaide Bartlett. He certainly enjoyed thoroughly being guide, philosopher, and friend to the couple, and until the catastrophe seems to have been amiable enough, if a little lacking in strength and character. According to his own story, he told Edwin at the time of the making of the will, that he was getting too fond of Adelaide, and suggested that he should discontinue seeing her. To this Edwin replied, in effect, "What are you fussing about?" and he made no further move. It would have demanded a greater effort than he was capable of to put an end to this pleasant, flattering, rather sentimental way of life; and it was not until the rude breath of publicity showed what the law would be likely to think of his conduct that he rushed to the opposite extreme, as is the way with the weak when stricken by panic. From that time, as we shall see, the Reverend George Dyson ceased to be either guide, philosopher, or friend to his former admirer.

Last, we come to the accused herself—Adelaide Bartlett, who is in some ways the most interesting of the three. Adelaide's photograph, taken at the age of thirty, shows a vigorous, dark young woman, with cropped curling hair, thick eyebrows, wide, dark eyes, and a full mouth—certainly a face of vigour and character. She was strong and healthy, having quite got over the illness which resulted from her pregnancy, fond of children, though she had none, and dogs, and enjoyed vigorous exercise. We are told that she was hot-tempered, and her face would bear out that possibility, though the only real evidence of it is that she quarrelled with her father-in-law and lost her temper with Dyson at a time when his pusillanimity must have been almost unendurable. She did not, apparently, lose her temper with Edwin during all the period of his illness, though that involved her in constant watching and in the performance of a large number of unpleasant duties. She was certainly a person of strong character and lively emotions, though not passionate in the erotic sense—at least, if she was, as Freudians may assert, her passions were assuredly not awakened. Whatever the truth about her marital relations with her husband, they were not passionate, and her relations with Dyson could hardly even have been termed philanderous. The other important fact about her is that she was practically friendless and occupationless, that this strong affectionate nature had until the arrival of Dyson nothing to expend itself on except a husband

who was continually at work. If she had had any sort of
job, or even a woman friend with whom she could spend
time and talk over her life, in all probability this history
would never have needed to be written. As things were,
she was almost bound to get bored and fidgety without
perhaps knowing why. We know that once in the early
days she became so exasperated that she left her husband's
house. We do not know how their relations stood at the
beginning of 1885; but it is at least conjecturable that Adelaide, after ten years of married life and no present or
likely outlet for her energies, was beginning to become
'edgy' and unreasonable, and that Edwin jumped at the
friendship of George Dyson as a means of making his wife
a useful companion without being a nuisance to him. His
whole attitude, in spite of his undoubted affection, bears
a certain resemblance to that of a man towards a pet dog
which he has bought when young, trained carefully and
taught to do tricks, and is prepared to treat kindly and
play with when he has time. If the pet dog develops a
personality of its own and becomes discontented, the pleasure in its possession becomes much less. The arrival of
George Dyson may very well have seemed to Edwin as a
godsend to enable his pet dog to be kept happy and
amused, and to prevent it from resenting his long absences
from home and his lack of adequate interest in the pet
dog's own avocations. Such an attitude may be unusual,
but it is hardly incredible.

Whatever the truth, right through the autumn of 1885
the parties were happy enough. Edwin had signed his new
will, which must greatly have pleased Adelaide, since under the old will she stood to be disinherited if she married
again after his death, and was known to have resented this
long before she met Dyson. (Even the Judge admitted that
he saw nothing discreditable to her in that; and fortunately

that particular form of tyranny seems to be now on the wane, though one of the strongest of the minor arguments for the doing away with inheritance is the great opportunity it gives to nasty old men and nasty old women for prolonging their nastinesses beyond the grave.)

The Bartletts left Dover and moved into lodgings in Claverton Street, Pimlico, in a house kept by one Frederick Doggett, who was also Registrar of Births, Marriages, and Deaths for the district; and asked as soon as possible to be provided with separate beds. (It was not unheard of, the Judge admitted, even in 1885, for married couples possessed of sufficient means to prefer not to occupy the same bed.) George Dyson was given a season ticket from Putney to Waterloo in order to enable him to continue his ministrations, and all seemed to be going well. But on December 8th Edwin Bartlett felt so ill at his work that he went home early; and from that time the troubles began. He never recovered from the illness, though he had ups and downs, and it continued till his sudden death some time in the night of New Year's Eve.

It was a most peculiar illness. Its cause was never diagnosed—it would almost seem, from the evidence, as though nobody ever asked about the cause; but its symptoms, as related by Dr. Leach, present a remarkable combination. Its chief characteristic, I venture to suggest after carefully reading all the evidence, was morbid hysteria, and I shall revert later to possible explanations of its inception. I do not mean to imply that there was nothing physically wrong with Edwin; obviously there was; but several of the symptoms, such as sleeplessness, were of a kind which hysteria would increase, and there is abundant evidence of despair, depression, curious fancies, and a desire to be fussed and made much of, continuing throughout its course. He liked to have his wife, for example, in constant attendance on him all the time; all through his illness she never undressed or went to bed herself, but slept in a chair at the foot of his bed, *holding his foot*, which seemed in some way to soothe him to sleep. On one occasion he told Dr. Leach that he had risen from his bed and stood for two hours over his sleeping wife drawing vital mesmeric force from her. Neither Dr. Leach nor Adelaide believed this statement, but that it should have been made shows the mental condition of the man. Dr. Leach, at all events, thought that the trouble lay in the mind as much as in the body, and half-way through the course of the illness was trying to persuade his patient to pull himself together and go for a holiday. "I wanted him to go to Torquay alone," he told the court. "He was practically a hysterical patient, and his wife petted him very much." Certainly Dr. Leach did not think that Edwin Bartlett's sufferings, however much they distressed him and exhausted his wife, were likely to end in death.

Whether they were or were not exaggerated by hysteria, Edwin's symptoms were unpleasant enough, as a bare recital will show. It was on December 8th that he went home ill from his office, and two days later, on the 10th, as he seemed really in a bad way, Adelaide sent for Dr. Alfred Leach, who lived just round the corner. Neither of the Bartletts had ever met Dr. Leach before; he was sent for because he happened to be the nearest doctor available. He came, and found Edwin suffering from vomiting, diarrhœa, severe pain in the side, hæmorrhage, nervous exhaustion, and sleeplessness. Naturally, with all these unpleasant conditions pursuing him, he was in a very low and gloomy condition; and he had a further symptom which perplexed Dr. Leach considerably. On looking into his mouth Dr. Leach saw a blue line around his gums, and formed the firm opinion that he was suffering from mercurial poisoning. He was so much impressed by this that he made an excuse to send Mrs. Bartlett out of the room, and then asked Edwin whether the presence of mercury was to be accounted for in the ordinary way—i.e. in plain language, whether he had been suffering from syphilis and had taken mercury as a remedy.

Edwin replied that he had not, and there were no signs of syphilis found in him either then or afterwards. As to the presence of mercury, he explained it by saying that he had taken a 'large pill' out of a drawer and eaten it. He could not remember whence or how he had procured this pill; and Dr. Leach, not unnaturally, seems to have formed the opinion that a man who could tell him such a story was either lying or incredibly foolish. However, he proceeded to treat him as best he could. He gave him bismuth, cinchona, and nux vomica, and a mouthwash of chlorate of potash and lemon syrup, as his mouth was in a very unpleasant condition. Edwin, however, continued ill, and on the next day Dr. Leach added to his prescription bicarbonate of soda, bromide of ammonium and tincture of chloroform. Three days later, on the 14th, he had an opium pill for his sleeplessness, and a different mouth lotion, and on the following day a preparation of gentian and nux vomica.

Still he remained ill, and when Dr. Leach visited him on the 16th he found him suffering, in addition to his other woes, from flatulence and great pain in the tongue and teeth. At this time the doctor examined his patient's mouth more closely—as he might well have done before—and found that his teeth were in a very bad condition. This was not surprising, for ten or eleven years previously Edwin Bartlett had had from a dentist a form of treatment which must, one hopes, have been unusual even sixty years ago. He had had most of his teeth sawn off, and artificial teeth put in to replace them, without the roots and stumps of the old teeth being removed. Old Mr. Bartlett, who provided the information about this operation, explained that the sawing-off was necessary "because his teeth were all stuck together". It was "a most exceptional treatment", as the Judge commented. Naturally, after this lapse of time, the roots and gums were in "a most horrible condition", and Dr. Leach promptly sent for a dentist called Roberts, who on the 16th took out two of the stumps, on the 17th about eleven, on the 21st four, and one more on the 31st. Mr. Roberts also, on the occasion of his first visit, confirmed Dr. Leach by finding traces of mercurial poisoning.

After the 17th Dr. Leach expected his patient to improve rapidly, though he continued to prescribe a variegated series of medicines for him. On the 18th he gave him a strong dose of Epsom salts and some bromide of ammonia with chloral hydrate; on the 19th and 20th he gave him more chloral hydrate and morphia, with on the latter day some bromide as well; and on the 22nd another mouth wash. Nevertheless, he thought his patient better and was beginning to urge him to get up and go out into the air. But Edwin Bartlett did not agree that he was better; he would not go out, and became very distressed, not to say tearful, at the thought of the doctor's ceasing to call on him. On the 19th a curious incident occurred. Edwin Bartlett asked Dr. Leach to get a second opinion. Not, he explained, because he felt any lack of confidence, but because "some people"—which could only have meant his father—were making unpleasant remarks about his wife's nursing. Dr. Leach called a Dr. Dudley, who came and concurred in the treatment.

Well, by the 21st Dr. Leach thought that there was nothing medically the matter with his patient and that "what

would have done him good would have been to have sent
him on a sea-trip, with no one to nurse him and hold his
toe and that sort of nonsense.'' One may guess, in fact,
that Dr. Leach was by this time wondering whether he
would not soon have Adelaide as well on his hands as a
patient. The toe-holding and ''that sort of nonsense'' had
now gone on for nearly a fortnight, quite long enough to
shake the endurance of one not used to the strain of sick
nursing.

But Edwin Bartlett never went on his sea-trip. Perhaps
he was not quite as recovered as Dr. Leach rather impa-
tiently surmised; at any rate he succeeded, on the 23rd,
in passing a lumbricoid worm, and this upset him considerably. In Dr. Leach's words, ''that threw everything back
again''. It is certainly distressing to discover that one is
suffering from worms; but only a very nervous patient
would leap, as Edwin Bartlett did, to the conviction that
there were worms wriggling up his throat. After his death
the doctors, at Dr. Leach's request, searched his body
carefully for worms, but there was never a trace of any but
the one that appeared on the 23rd.

But that one was an undeniable worm, and had to be
treated. So on the 26th, having on the previous day tried
a new tonic containing phosphate of strychnine, he was
given a vermifuge, composed of santonine, sulphate of
soda and Urwick's extract; and in order that he might not
be too uncomfortable he was told to expel it with a draught
of sulphate of magnesium and tincture of jalap. This he
took, and followed it up on his own responsibility with
two globules of croton oil. Now croton oil is a very strong
purge. Attendants in badly run lunatic asylums have frequently got into trouble for using croton oil to keep their
patients weak and pliant; and one would accordingly have
had expected it to have at any rate some effect on Edwin

Bartlett. But not a bit—this remarkable patient only observed that it gave him a warm, comfortable feeling; and though Dr. Leach fed him on hot tea and coffee and applied galvanism to his abdomen, still nothing happened. Then Dr. Leach gave up in despair; but it would seem, notwithstanding his fears, that Edwin was able to absorb worm-powders easily into his system, for after this his health began to improve again, and on the 30th Dr. Leach again suggested discontinuing his attendance. Mrs. Bartlett begged him not to, "because it makes him so distressed"; and to this entreaty he agreed, and, further, made arrangements for Edwin to have yet another tooth taken out on the following day. By this time he had begun to suspect that Edwin was suffering from incipient necrosis of the jaw.

So we come to the last day of Edwin Bartlett's life—a day on which, although he had a tooth out under gas, he appeared to be in better spirits than he had been for some time. Not only was he in better spirits; he had also managed to acquire a fairly tolerable appetite, for, in spite of his encounter with the dentist, he succeeded in putting away oysters, jugged hare, bread and butter, cake, mango chutney, and more oysters. He told his landlady, after the jugged hare, that he could eat three such dinners every day; and almost his last recorded utterance registered his intention of getting up an hour earlier at the thought of having a large haddock for breakfast.

At four in the morning of New Year's Day Mr. Doggett was woken by Adelaide Bartlett, who told him that her husband was dead. He came up, found Edwin dead in bed, and the fire burning brightly, as though it had recently been mended. (I have mentioned this point because it received great stress from the prosecution, though how putting more coal on the fire could prove Adelaide Bartlett a murderess, I confess I am unable to understand. If she woke up, as she said, and found Edwin's foot cold in her hands, surely to mend the fire would be a very natural action. Everyone is not necessarily dead who has cold feet; they may even, perhaps, be suffering from cold, if the fire has died down.)

Dr. Leach was summoned, and confirmed the death, feeling very puzzled. At the earliest possible opportunity, Adelaide sent off telegrams to old Mr. Bartlett, Mr. Matthews, and Mr. Baxter, the dead man's partner—not, it should be observed, to George Dyson. Mr. Bartlett, when he came, was obviously bristling with suspicions. He smelt his dead son's lips for signs of prussic acid poisoning, declared that there was something wrong about the death and that the police must be sent for, and began feeling in the pockets of Adelaide's cloak to see if she had hidden anything there. He also kissed her, which even the Judge felt was going rather far.

The upshot was that it was felt that there must be a post-mortem—a decision in which Adelaide eagerly concurred—and an inquest. A police officer arrived to search the rooms, but his search was rather perfunctory, and he might have missed quite a number of things.

The post-mortem was held on January 2nd, and, greatly to Dr. Leach's surprise, though no definite conclusions were reached, it was found that some of the organs smelt strongly of chloroform. Subsequent analysis established that Edwin had died of chloroform poisoning in the stomach. Dr. Leach promptly communicated this fact to Adelaide, expecting that it would set her mind at rest; but, again to his surprise—throughout these events, poor Dr. Leach was continually being surprised—he found that he had caused her considerable distress. The post-mortem had already caused even more distress to the Reverend George Dyson, as will shortly appear.

Where had the chloroform come from? There was no chloroform to be seen, though Dr. Leach looked around for it, and among all his variegated drugging of Edwin, his doctor had never prescribed pure chloroform. The explanation, at the coroner's court, which was held early in February, was provided by George Dyson.

George Dyson told the court that on December 27th Mrs. Bartlett had privately asked him to buy her some chloroform in order that she might use it to quieten her husband, who in the course of his illness suffered from violent internal paroxysms. She added that, as she would have to administer the chloroform by sprinkling it upon a handkerchief which she would wave in front of his face, and as chloroform was extremely volatile, she would have to have a fairly large quantity of the drug. When Dyson asked why she could not get it through the doctor, she replied that the doctor would not believe that she was "skilled in the administration of chloroform".

Whether he believed this tale or not—we must, I think, in view of his evident anxiety to save his skin, believe that it was substantially the tale which he was told—Dyson was sufficiently under the influence of the stronger character to do as he was asked. He bought the chloroform, in four separate purchases, lying as to the reason for which it was wanted, but making no other attempt to cover his actions; and on the 29th, having emptied his four bottles into one, handed the big bottle to Adelaide. That bottle was never seen again. The police officer who searched the room failed to find it; old Mr. Bartlett is our witness that it was not concealed in Adelaide's cloak. Adelaide herself said that at a later stage she threw it, empty, into a pond; but nobody found it.

Not unnaturally, when Dyson heard on January 2nd that the dead man's organs had smelt of chloroform, he was horribly frightened. On the next morning he threw away his little bottles on Wimbledon Common, where one of them was subsequently found by the police. At the earliest possible opportunity he tackled Adelaide and asked her what she had done with the chloroform. She replied: "Oh, damn the chloroform!" and stamped her foot at him. Nevertheless he remained agitated, and on other occasions cross-questioned her in no friendly manner. He cried out: "I am a ruined man!" and consulted a friend, who wisely counselled him to wait until the results of the analysis were known, and not go wildly dashing off to the police. Neither this counsel nor his running round in circles availed him much, for at the inquest the jury which returned a verdict against Adelaide Bartlett found that the Reverend George Dyson had been an accessory after the fact. When the trial came on, however, it was observed that the Crown had decided not to proceed against him, but to use him as a witness. It was suggested that this was fortunate for Adelaide, since it enabled her counsel to cross-examine him; it should, however, be remarked that the Crown advisers presumably knew what they were about, and valued the testimony that they could get by allowing Dyson to give evidence.

The explanation—if there be an explanation—of the whole tragedy falls into two parts: the administration of the poison, and the condition of things which led up to it. Sir Edward Clarke, who defended Adelaide, decided— quite rightly, as he was dealing with the law—that the former aspect, which to my mind is far the less interesting, was the one on which to concentrate; and, accordingly, much time was spent in disputing how the chloroform could have got into Edwin Bartlett's stomach.

There was, of course, more than one way in which this might have happened. The prosecution, rather unfortunately for themselves, based their case throughout on the theory that Adelaide Bartlett killed her husband by first stupefying him as he slept and then pouring the rest of the poison down his throat; and Sir Edward Clarke, who had given much more study to the scientific side of the problem than had his Crown opponent, had no difficulty at all in showing that such an operation would have been one of extraordinary subtlety, and would have needed either remarkable skill or remarkable good fortune to enable it to be successfully performed. The prosecution tried to make much of the fact that in the house there was a copy of a work of reference, Squire's *Companion to the British Pharmacopœia*, which appeared to open naturally at the pages dealing with chloroform. They suggested that it was from this book that Adelaide derived the knowledge which enabled her to commit her crime; but Sir Edward Clarke observed that even if she had studied it with all care, all that she would have found out was that chloroform was volatile—which would not have helped her much.

I do not propose to follow in detail all the lengthy evidence which was given by the medical witnesses. The net effect was that, while the doctors were not prepared to swear that it would be impossible to commit murder by these means, they all thought it was highly unlikely. There appeared to have been only one authentic case in the whole course of medical history of the successful chloroforming of a patient during sleep—and he was a boy of sixteen, and not a grown man in a nervous and hysterical condition. It was this great improbability that saved Adelaide Bartlett; if the prosecution could have thought in time of any more plausible way in which she could have administered the poison she would certainly have been convicted.

If that hypothesis were ruled out as too difficult, there were various others. There was accident—but that also was highly unlikely. Liquid chloroform burns and causes violent pain; if Edwin had drunk liquid chloroform in mistake for something else he would certainly not have died without mentioning the fact. The theory that the defence in its closing speech put up was that Edwin Bartlett committed suicide, that in despair of enjoying life again he turned his face to the wall and drank off the chloroform. This theory, like the suggestion subsequently published by Dr. Leach, that he drank the poison to annoy his wife, and accidentally drank too much, involved consideration of the relationship of the Bartletts, and must for the moment be deferred.

Finally, the last speech of the advocate for the Crown hinted that there was another means by which murder might have been committed. Suppose that Adelaide Bartlett, whose care and scrupulousness as a nurse her husband had never had any reason to doubt, had handed him the chloroform to drink, suggesting, perhaps, that it was a new medicine guaranteed to make him sleep. Would he not have taken it from her hand, and might he not have swallowed it down before he realized that he was drinking poison? The Judge, in his summing-up, ruled this explanation out of order. It had not been made in time and according to the proper forms, and therefore, by the rules of the law game, the jury must not pay any attention to it. So they did not; but if the learned Attorney-General had realized rather earlier that his first hypothesis was going to fall down on him, things might not have gone so well for his prisoner. The law is a curious beast; it is not really interested to find out what did happen, or why, but whether a theory put forward by one party to the dispute can or cannot be proved according to the rules.

Leaving for the moment the question how the chloroform got into Edwin Bartlett, let us consider for a while how it came to be in his room at all. We know the actual physical means by which it got there; it was bought at four separate shops by George Dyson and given to Adelaide Bartlett at her request. But for what purpose did she want it?

Here we come on to more difficult ground. We do not know from Adelaide herself why she wanted it, for did she not give evidence, on the advice of her lawyers, either at the inquest or at the trial. We have to rely upon stories told by Dyson and by Dr. Leach, both of whom the Judge thought highly unreliable witnesses, and we have the further difficulty that the stories themselves, as far as they concern the relations between the Bartletts, come under the heading of 'subjective truth', that is, we may believe that they adequately represent the emotional situation without necessarily being correct in all details.

Adelaide, on January 26th, after the analysis had shown death to be due to chloroform poisoning, came to Dr. Leach, and told him in confidence, as her private physician, what must have been almost the full history of her married life. She began by saying that she was married at sixteen. This was one of the details that was certainly not true, though she seems to have been so undeveloped at the time of her marriage that she may very well have felt like sixteen, even though she was three years older. But, she said, her husband had always had peculiar ideas about marriage, and when they married it was on the understanding that there should be no intercourse between them. This rule was kept, even after she returned from her convent school to live in her husband's house, and was only broken once, when she petitioned to be allowed to have a child. But the child died, as we know; and after that they resumed their platonic relations, sharing the same bed for years, but without being lovers. They always got on very well, she said, except on one occasion, when they quarrelled about old Mr. Bartlett's treatment of her: it was then that she ran away.

But during the last few months of his life, she said, and after they had become so friendly with George Dyson, Edwin's nature seemed to change, and he wanted to lay claim to the rights which he had had for ten years but never exercised. She resisted; she told him that "he had practically made her over to George Dyson", and that it was not fair now, suddenly, to demand to be her husband in the full sense. As to what the phrase quoted meant, or meant to Adelaide, we are rather in the dark. Dr. Leach does not seem to have pressed for an explanation; nor did the court. It did not mean that Dyson was her lover, for he was not. The only direct light that is thrown upon it is Bartlett's will naming Dyson as executor, and a conversation which Dyson had with him some time in October concerning Adelaide, in the course of which Dyson said to him, "If ever she comes under my care I shall have to teach her differently," or some such words. Dyson made it quite clear that in his opinion Edwin certainly intended his friend and his wife to come together after his death, even if he did not say so definitely. Of course, that is not quite the same thing as "making her over" during his lifetime; but it is not so far off.

At all events Adelaide did not at all want to live with Edwin as his wife, and did her best to make that plain. The decision to take separate beds on the move to Claverton Street fits in obviously with this part of her story. But Edwin was not moved by her objections. The more ill he got the more he seemed to want to make love to her, and this at a time when she was becoming exhausted and worn by sick-nursing. So at last she conceived a plan to stupefy him when he began to make these advances, by soaking a handkerchief in chloroform and waving it in his face; and for this purpose she got Dyson to buy her some chloroform, giving him another reason for wanting it, as she was too shy to give him the real one. Dr. Leach, to whom she poured all this out on January 26th, remarked that if she had tried the experiment, she would probably have upset the bottle and chloroformed them both.

But she never tried it. The bottle worried her, she said, lying there in her drawer, and on New Year's Eve, when Edwin was lying in his bed, she made confession. She told him all about it, and gave him the bottle, which was corked but not full. "He was not cross; we talked amicably and seriously, and he turned round on his side and pretended to go to sleep, or to sulk, or something of that sort." (It was this part of her story which caused the defence to suggest that Edwin might have killed himself.) Then she left him with the bottle beside him, changed her clothes, and composed herself to sleep at the foot of the bed. She heard him snoring violently, but took no notice; and when she woke at four in the morning, he was dead. She could not say whether any chloroform had disappeared from the bottle; but she took it and hid it somewhere, and at a later date threw it into Peckham Rye Pond. It was not found there; but neither was it found anywhere else.

Now, what is one to make of all this? Mr. Justice Wills thought it a farrago of indecent nonsense, and Dr. Leach a fool for believing any of it, as he obviously did. But is it really so incredible? Plenty more people, even in 1885, had curious lives than ever came into court.

It is pretty certain that Edwin and Adelaide Bartlett married upon platonic terms, that, whether or no the statement about their never having lived together as man and wife was strictly accurate—it all depends exactly what you mean or exactly what Adelaide meant by 'living together'—their mode of life had very little in it that was sexual, and that this mode of life suited Edwin excellently until two or three months before his death. Adelaide was inclined to be bored; psycho-analysts will no doubt say that the boredom was due purely to the lack of a full sex life. But if it was, she certainly did not know it, and she was quite happy again when George Dyson turned up. She did not want to sleep with him. I myself think that, like a good many women, she did not want to sleep with anybody; quite possibly the episode of the baby that died had given her a horror of the whole thing. But she did very much enjoy being petted and made a fuss of, and to have a little superior culture offered her. Edwin, until about October, also approved of the arrangement very well. He liked to have Adelaide kept amused and happy while he was away, by a young man for whom he had conceived a great and almost embarrassing admiration, who regarded him with friendship and affection, and was always ready to discuss and to offer advice. It seems fairly clear, whatever the Judge thought about it, that he did contemplate George and Adelaide marrying if he should die.

But during the last months of his life something changed in Edwin Bartlett. It is difficult to be sure what that was or why it happened; but there are various points to be noted. In the first place, he was just over forty, an age when men are notoriously apt to suffer sex-changes, if only temporarily. Mostly, men go off the rails; Edwin seems to have gone *on* the rails, though with no less unfortunate effects. Secondly, he was definitely overworking; his body, therefore, was ripe for a breakdown of some sort as soon as his mind would concede it, and his old teeth had probably been poisoning him for some time. So, I suggest, he began to feel sorry for himself, and probably also to feel, at the back of his mind, that Adelaide was getting rather too much interested in the playmate he had found her, and that master was getting a little bit pushed out. At any rate, the whole course of his illness suggests an attempt to get into the middle of the picture, and to keep his wife busy about him. He wants her to be with him all the time, to hold his toe, and generally feed him with her own vitality. Sometimes he'll feel better, sometimes worse; but all the time he is in such a mental state as to demand her continual attention.

Then, on top of all this, he wants to possess her as he has never possessed her before. The Judge found it quite incredible that this desire should have come upon him while he was ill. I do not find it so. In the first place, sexual desire is not in the least incompatible with a certain amount of bodily discomfort, and he was not at any time really disablingly ill. He had not, for instance, a high fever. Secondly, I submit that there are one or two facts, which were not all disclosed at the trial, which suggest that Adelaide's disclosures to Dr. Leach did not cover the whole facts of her husband's life. After his death, there were found, not in a box or anywhere like that, but in his trouser pocket, a number of French letters. This is fact number one. Fact number two is that he undoubtedly suggested more than once that a man ought to be allowed two wives—one for companionship, and one, as it were, for use. Adelaide, we know, was the companion. And fact number three is that both Dr. Leach and the dentist, at the beginning of his last illness, found him suffering from mercurial poisoning—and he gave no credible explanation of how the mercury could have got inside him. Do not these three facts require some explanation? And is it not at least a possible explanation that Edwin Bartlett, through the ten years of his married life, was platonic with his wife while finding natural satisfaction elsewhere, that in the October or November he got a nasty fright which caused him to forswear outside amusements, and that thenceforward he was intending to take Adelaide for use as well as companionship? That suggestion would remove some of the learned Judge's difficulties.

I do not suggest that Adelaide would have been aware of his previous habits or of the reason for the change. Whether she was or was not, I find no difficulty in understanding that the change was extremely distasteful to her. As I have said, she did not want to sleep with anybody, and Edwin, in his condition at the time, can hardly have been an attractive lover. Besides, she was extremely tired, probably near hysteria herself, and certainly in no condition to deal with the sudden new strain. For Adelaide, as I read her, was a person of courage and vitality, but inclined to be impatient and not very good at standing strains. She had been doing an altogether ridiculous amount of nursing, and she was the kind of person who, being in excellent health, light-heartedly undertakes a long, exhausting and unpleasant job without in the least realizing the extent to which it can fray one's nerves. That is the type which, without warning, suddenly cracks—and she had nobody to help her. She did not have the 'time off' which any professional nurse would have had; she had no intimate women friends, and it was not possible, even under the circumstances, for her to discuss this particular problem with Dyson—not that it was likely to help her much if she had; for if ever there was a broken reed it was that young Wesleyan minister. Even her doctor was stranger, and her husband's father an enemy.

So she bought the chloroform, and I think it quite likely that the reason she gave to Dr. Leach was a true reason, and that she had some sort of vague idea that she might be able to choke Edwin off if he became too affectionate. I think it is certainly more probable than that she intended to pour it down his throat. Beyond that we do not know. Her account of her last conversation with Edwin may have been true. He may have subsequently, in a fit of despair—possibly a fit of indigestion, which he well deserved—have drunk off the poison, or he may have swallowed it, intending to get a little more attention. Both these explanations involve some difficulties; both suggest that the final conversation, whatever it may have been about, was not really amicable. And it is very difficult to believe that, in either event, Edwin died without making a sound that would disturb his wife.

It may be that her control, in the middle of the night, suddenly broke and that she persuaded him either to drink the chloroform or to allow himself to be stupefied so that she could pour it down. If that was so, the real breaking-point came, I suggest, when Dr. Leach informed her that he was practically recovered and was suffering from nothing but hysteria. For hysteria is neither fatal nor easily cured, and the prospect of Edwin living with her another thirty years or so, off and on, in that condition might well have seemed too appalling to face. If, after spending a day eating heartily and appearing better, he developed another attack of melancholia and affection late at night, one can see that it might have been the last straw, and that she might have taken one of those insane decisions which strong characters, strained too hard and left too much to their own resources, do sometimes come to in the middle of the night. Luckily, they do not often have the means of action ready to hand. Adelaide Bartlett had.

This much is clear. She knew, or half knew, even before the post-mortem, that the bottle of chloroform had something to do with her husband's death. If she did not kill him, she felt herself guilty of some neglect or other—perhaps she had simply resolved to go to sleep and take no notice of any noise he made; she must have been sleepy enough. If she did kill him, she did not properly realize it. She had only, as it were, emotionally willed his death, and had not taken in that her pipe dream was a reality. Hence her clamour for a post-mortem and her rage at Dyson's fears. It must have been a sudden, half-insane impulse. But if the jury had been allowed to consider the possibility of her 'having poisoned Edwin with his own partial co-operation, she would never have gone free—because she was odd, and because she had a book on birth-control. So possibly, though by curious ways, justice was in the end served.

PART IV

Business as Usual
An Impression of the Landru Case

by E. R. Punshon

I   The Murderer as Man of Affairs

DURING that four-year feast of horror and terror we remember as the war, there were few phrases aroused an indignation more general than the recommendation of a certain German diplomat that neutral ships engaged in trade with the Allies should be 'sunk without trace'. About such total disappearance indeed there is always a quality both of mystery and dread that seems to affect the mind to a peculiar degree. The chances of fate we are all aware that we must reckon with. Death itself all know, and know that all must face in time; its portals may be awful, but they are familiar, and from the familiar there has always been taken away something at least of the terrible.

But when what happens is simply that our place and habitation knows us no longer, when we are not and none can tell why, when no spot of earth can be pointed to as our last resting-place, when the veil of the unknown covers all with such obscurity that even the actual fact of death can only be surmised, not proved, then indeed in such a fate there is felt to be an element of terror unique in its own degree of poignancy, when to the mystery of death is added the mystery of the unknown.

Thus is the story of events that passed not so many years ago, the mystery of complete and utter disappearance which befell in the midst of a great and crowded city, a long succession of eleven people—ten women and a boy— seems to set the tale quite apart in the sad category of crime. Others have killed as remorselessly, others have claimed as many victims or more, only Henri Désiré Landru succeeded in concealing so completely the fate of his victims, that concerning it nothing can be declared with certainty. Indeed, it is not too much to say that, in each case considered apart and by itself, conviction would have been impossible. No jury could have been asked to bring in a verdict of guilty had each case stood alone. No proof existed that the supposed victims were even dead, nothing to show they had not simply gone about their business, as Landru protested that they had, and were not, as his advocate suggested, quietly living somewhere or another ignorant even of the accusation brought against their supposed murderer and, therefore, not coming forward to show themselves and prove his innocence.

But if in logic it is impossible to add eleven probabilities together to make one certainty; if, in law, case 'A' should always be considered without reference to case 'B'; life, even in France, is more than either logic or law. Of late years, too, scientists have made us aware of what they call 'statistical laws', telling us that, for example, if the table we were sitting at vanished at some moment from our ken, that would be no miracle but merely the result of a quite conceivable accident, that of all the violently circulating molecules composing the table chancing to find themselves all in one spot at one moment. But that is as unlikely as that all the inhabitants of London should chance to decide to take a walk down Fleet Street at the same hour of the same afternoon, even though such a decision is quite conceivable of each one of them taken separately. So, though in each case of these disappearances wherein Landru stands convicted, absolute proof is lacking, yet when with a monotonous and dreadful regularity it is shown that he was the last person with whom the missing individual was seen and after that was seen no more, then it may be claimed there is achieved that complete certainty which is above all proof, since proof must always rest upon premise that must in its turn be proved, and so on, indefinitely.

Of the eleven people whose strange fate is was thus to be, as it were, annihilated, there is not much to be said, for they were all of them just those who form the vast majority of mankind—the *tout le monde* in French, the 'Everyman' or rather 'Everywoman' in English, the neighbours, fellow-citizens, the casual passers-by with whom we all rub shoulders as we go to and fro about our daily business. None of them could have dreamed, busy as they were with their own concerns, so trivial to the rest of us, so significant and important to themselves, that the Fates had flung for them dice marked with a doom so dreadfully unknown.

For the most part they were middle-aged women, widows or elderly spinsters, though one was a lad of eighteen or twenty, and another, seen hovering for a moment on the outskirts of the tragedy before it engulfed her too, was a young girl. She was an orphan apparently. She seems to have had not a friend or a relative in the world, she had no money, she had nothing to attract attention in looks or talent or education, nothing to suggest the strange doom awaiting her. She seemed inevitably destined for the quiet, laborious life of the average working girl, possibly with marriage in the future or some small, modest niche in the world she would be able to make or find for herself. We have the merest glimpse of her, gathering flowers, enjoying the fresh country air at Gambais, near the Forest of Rambouillet, chattering with her 'uncle', as she called Landru, using his pet name in talking to him, and then passing into the unknown, no more to be seen or heard of, leaving us to guess in vain why or how.

Surely the very extremity of wantonness to take a child as harmless, as indifferent, as a mouse behind the skirting-board, and ere yet her life had well begun involve her in so dark and strange a tragedy.

It is in 1915 that the story begins, so far at least as is known, though prologues as yet unheard of there may well have been. They were days when the world, in its madness, was tearing itself to pieces, when the foolish mumbling of the guns could be plainly heard in quiet weather on the Surrey downs, and yet when, as it is a little hard to remember, the business of daily life had still to go on as usual, when buying and selling, eating and drinking, rising up in the morning and lying down at night had still to continue.

'Business as usual' had indeed come into its own; unhappy phrase invented at the beginning of the war by those who imagined that war was still conducted under the limited liability act; then becoming a term of reproach for failure to understand that when the house burned nothing mattered but extinguishing the flames; then coming back into a tacit acceptance, as it was realized that even in the midst of terrors hitherto undreamed of the daily trivialities still kept their place, and that each morning tea and toast still bulked as largely in the daily economy as tidings of defeat and victory and lists of casualties whole columns long.

'Business as usual', then, and no one pursued this ideal more thoroughly than Henri Désiré, going briskly, methodically, industriously about his business, though indeed what that business was none of those dreamed who sat by him in train or tram, passed him in the street, bargained with him for the purchase of the certainly rather peculiar odds and ends, the bits of furniture, and so on, he had at times to dispose of. Occasionally, too, smart and confident, he would step into a bank or a broker's office with government bonds or share certificates he had to dispose of, formerly the property of a Madame This or That, widow or spinster, as the case might be, and now recently come into his possession.

And always he had his note-book ready to hand, so that everything might be jotted down and nothing forgotten or overlooked. A man indeed who understood routine and made of it murder's accepted servant, a man to whom method and routine were necessary since, in addition to his chief business of assassination, he had so many other things to think of, a man to whom method was so much a habit that, though one might think the exact hour of a murder was not easily forgotten on the one hand, or on the other hand its record either prudent or important, was yet obliged to jot it down, day, hour, and minute all carefully recorded in that same note-book with all the other details of daily engagements and expenses—so much for a bus fare, this hour for meeting a friend to drink with him a glass of wine, or a cup of coffee, for Landru was a sober man; that hour for the completion of the latest murder!

No wonder that to all who came in contact with him he seemed the very type of the busy, careful, efficient man of affairs, smiling and cheerful, his pleasant, gentle manner covering a keen business sense.

"I know well how to claim my commission," he said of himself later on.

A man diligent in his affairs shall stand before kings; there is Scriptural authority for believing, and for Henri Désiré Landru, whose diligence none could doubt, the promise was destined to prove as true as might be in a republic, for if he never came to stand before kings, at any rate, presently, he was to stand up in a court!

In general, his chief dealings were in furniture, but he traded in motors also, and indeed in anything that presented itself for sale or purchase. He was tenant, too, of a small garage, and as befitted a methodical man of business, he was always punctual in paying his rent and other charges—in fact all through his queer history of fraud and murder there is no suggestion that he ever failed to meet his daily obligations. What he owed he paid, even to the final payment one morning in a Versailles square. Probably to his precise and punctual mind a debt was a worry, but a swindle or a murder merely a business transaction, popular prejudice made it necessary to carry out in private. He owned, too, a kind of light lorry he used for conveying recent acquisitions to this garage, where presently an unsympathetic police, rummaging and searching, were to find such things as the false hair of women, who, according to Landru, had parted from him to go travelling in foreign countries; the identity papers of little servant girls who, according to Landru, had left him to seek for fresh posts they would have no chance of obtaining without those papers; the cherished trifles, china ornaments, and so on, elderly widows had clung to all their lives till now when, according to Landru, they had confided them to him, before departing about their business; small pieces of family jewellery that had been the pride of equally elderly spinsters and their proof of social standing, but that now, too, had found their way to the garage where was stored this strange collection, almost every item once the property of a woman who once had known Landru and now was known to none.

In fact it seems as if about this time any insertion in a Paris newspaper of what in France is called a *petite annonce*, in England a 'small classified', offering furniture for sale, would be apt to bring the pleasant, smiling, soft-spoken, confidence-creating Landru to the door, ready to make an offer all the more liberal, since his intention was to pay otherwise than in cash.

And how could the anxious, slightly flustered, slightly worried middle-aged woman, anxious to secure for her possession the best price possible—how could she dream that the step upon her stairs of this prospective purchaser was the step of Death in Mystery, that when she opened the door to his soft knock, it was that soon she might pass through that open door to a doom none would ever know?

Fantastic such an idea would have seemed and yet so it was to be, not once alone, but time after time, one after another in the most tragic, singular procession surely the world has ever seen—this long line of drab, work-worn, middle-aged, quiet, saving women passing from the warm security of the little homes they had made for themselves to an enigmatic fate a whole world would presently discuss and all the skill and effort of the police of France fail to elucidate.

The beginning indeed is clear enough. The start of the affair can easily be reconstructed, from imagination only, it is true, since no record is there to be consulted, but on a foundation of reasonable, almost certain conjecture, so that the picture forms itself as plainly as though before an eye-witness.

Nearly always the start is the *petite annonce*. Sometimes it is one that Landru, always a great patron of the *petite annonce*, inserts, offering to buy furniture. Occasionally it is an announcement of furniture that for some reason some woman wished to dispose of. Or it takes the form of a matrimonial advertisement, couched in the queer abbreviated form the economical French love to employ, with Landru in the character of the business man possessing a small capital and seeking wife and partner with savings to match his own.

One can so easily imagine the hesitations and the doubts with which the insertion or the reading of these advertisements would be accomplished, how carefully they would be considered, how prudently the final decision would be arrived at, that at any rate there could be no harm in finding out what this unknown monsieur had to say for himself or what price he would be prepared to offer for whatever was to be sold.

Writing materials are sought, therefore; a letter composed with care and difficulty, for one does not write a letter every day, it is dropped into the post, there is an answer, and the Angel of Death comes leading to the door that gentle, quiet-spoken Landru, in whom one has confidence from the start, so favourable is the instant impression that he makes.

Only the very faintest knowledge of the psychology of the average lower middle-class Frenchwoman is needed to understand with what suspicion and hostility the advent of this potential buyer had been awaited. One had been prepared for all, one had expected every effort to beat down prices to the lowest possible figure. Instead, here was this polite, smiling, gentle man, *un vrai monsieur,* so liberal in his views, willing to offer a price better than could have been dreamed of, and above all much more interested apparently in oneself than in one's possessions.

As the presiding magistrate remarked to Landru later on: "It seems it was your habit to enter as a client, to emerge as a *fiancé.*"

The tale he told no doubt varied in every instance. As the flood of refugees poured into Paris from the invaded regions, he became one of them. He had enormous claims against the State for his factory in Lille occupied by the Germans. Or he had rendered immense services to the State, for which he was to be rewarded by an appointment as consul in Australia. Or else it was Brazil, where the future domicile was to be established, and as it was obviously impossible to think of taking one's furniture to Brazil or Australia, it had better be sold and Landru could obtain the best possible price. Sometimes the stories were not so precise, no doubt Landru doled them out according to the probable credulity of the listener. Inquiries about the consular appointments in Australia or commercial enterprises in Brazil can be made in the appropriate quarters. Questions may even be asked about factories said to have flourished in the invaded districts, and though the solitary and ill-educated women whom Landru sought out were credulous enough, yet even they might still have friends to make awkward inquiries. But in war time important secret service rendered to the State is a safe card to play, and Landru appears to have employed it more than once. Even so, doubts seem to have been aroused occasionally, and 'Mr. Mystery' was the name given him by the acquaintance of at least one of his victims, though whether the name was bestowed in admiration or in suspicion, or perhaps in a mingling of both, does not seem too clear.

The details, then, would vary with the circumstances. No exact information is to be obtained, except in each case from what the concierge remembered of confidences made to her, for it is noticeable that all these women led such lonely lives, with relatives so few or so distant, that it was only to the concierge they were able to gossip about the charming gentleman who had so unexpectedly come into their lives, of his attentions and unfailing kindness, his courtesy, and the happy prospects opening out before them. In one or two cases when friends might have wondered why Madame So-and-So had cut herself off from them so entirely, Landru took pains to send a box of chocolates as a parting present, or flowers—he had always a weakness for flowers—that had come ostensibly all the way from Nice, where it was to be assumed the lady was happily and comfortably installed in her new life. Impossible to suppose that harm had come to one who took the trouble to send such lovely flowers in such profusion all the way from the South of France.

But if the details varied, the end was the same. A little trip to the country would be proposed, a pleasant excursion, such as town-dwellers love all the world over, and Parisians perhaps more than most. There was a little villa at Vernouillet, small and pleasant town in the valley of the Seine. Later it was another small villa, the Villa Tric, as it was called from the landlord's name, in the lonely village of Gambais, on the outskirts of the forest of Rambouillet, not very far from where in that same forest every morning a fleet of lorries from Paris deposits fresh tons of the refuse of the great city in enormous pits and disused quarries that exist there, and that the authorities have adopted this method of filling in.

A careful and far-seeing man like Landru, so cautious and so calculating, may possibly have noticed this, have watched with interest in the early morning that long line of lorries issuing fully laden from Paris and returning empty, and have perceived that from this public enterprise some private profit might be drawn.

At any rate it was in Gambais that the idyll, begun when a prospective purchaser of furniture called in answer to an advertisement at a small Paris flat, would presently draw to its conclusion.

One morning Landru and Madame—there are ten names that can be filled in at choice—would set out, Landru, one is sure, as smiling and attentive and polite as ever, and Madame—take which name you prefer from the list—one can well imagine, in high spirits at the prospects of this country jaunt with the *vrai monsieur* who had power to depict their joint future in such glowing colors and who, for proof of his position in the world, was able to boast of the reality of the favourite dream of the Parisian—a little villa in the country.

She would be quite content to wait while he left her for a moment to buy their tickets and presently he would return still smiling and attentive as ever, with the tickets, one single and one return.

A thoughtful man, it is to be noted, and one with an eye to detail. Why go to the unnecessary expense of buying a return ticket for one who would not return?

Carefully he would enter the details in his note-book, jotting down exactly how much for the single ticket, how much for the return, while no doubt Madame looked on admiringly, and with true French love of thrift thought how fortunate she was to have found a man who knew so well how to look after his sous.

Here, for instance, are the items of the expenses for one such day copied directly from his note-book, his careful note-book, for April 4, 1918:

	Fr.
Garage voiture	1.00
Figues 1.80 + .45 rembourse de valise............	2.25
Voiture, Invalides, 3.00, billets, 3.10 & 4.95....	11.05
1 pneumatique à 7h. 0.40..............................	.40
Diligence...	2.40

The price for a single ticket from Paris to the nearest
station to the village of Gambais—a diligence running between the station and the village—being at that time three
francs ten, or a return ticket four francs ninety-five.

Grotesquely, and a little horribly, reminiscent, is it not,
of the old legendary tag of duelling days: ''Pistols for two;
coffee for one''?

And there the story ends so far as any facts are known.
It was a Madame Pascal to whom these special entries
referred. She had been a dressmaker, earning a comfortable, if modest living. On that morning of April 4, 1918,
Landru called at her small flat, and with him she left for
the country trip they had planned together. At the railway
station he bought, as duly entered in his note-book, one
single ticket and one return. Since then, since that hour
when she left her flat with Landru, the man whose 'charming courtesy', whose 'perfect breeding' she had so often
praised to friends, she had never more been seen, nor has
any recognizable trace of her been found. That April 4th
she stepped out of the ranks of the living to be no more
heard of, and the next day, April 5th, Landru, content and
tranquil, returned alone to Paris, having first in his careful, precise, business-like manner jotted down in his note-
book the small expenses of the previous day such items as
the purchase of a cup of coffee, a roll, tobacco, and so on.
Also there is noted in larger, clearer figures, at the top of
the page for that day the hours of five-fifteen in the eve-

ning, though with no indication of what event it was he considered interesting enough to record in this manner.

Within a week, having entered into possession of Madame Pascal's flat, he had sold her furniture and her personal belongings, and so was her tale done, till it began to be retold again in a court-room at Versailles.

Yet how within that brief space of time between, say, a quarter-past five in the evening and Landru's presentation at the station for Gambais of the return ticket to Paris with which he had so thoughtfully provided himself, did he manage and contrive so successfully to dispose of Madame Pascal's body that no trace remained, no sign of struggle, no bloodstains to be found, no cry heard, nothing?

A busy and efficient man this Henri Désiré Landru seems to have been, that much praise at least he has fairly earned.

II The Murderer Domestic

At this time Landru, born in 1869, and therefore in middle age, was a man to all appearance *rangé*, as the French say. His parents seem to have been, to quote the story books, "poor but honest". The father is described as a *mécanicien*, a rather vague term that might cover any occupation from that of driving an express on one of the railways to casual stoking in the boiler-house of any factory. Probably the civil state of Landru senior was more akin to the latter occupation than to the former. Nothing is recorded to his discredit and, indeed, nothing to remark on his life save his method of quitting it, for he committed suicide in the Bois de Boulogne in 1912. It is no doubt far-fetched to suggest that the motive for this suicide may have been his realization of the kind of monster he had brought into the world. His wife in the usual thrifty French fashion helped the family income by doing needlework. So far as is known there is nothing in the family history to suggest any taint of degeneracy or disease. In his childhood, too, Landru appears to have made a good impression. He became a choir boy which certainly would not have happened had anything serious been known to his discredit, and his taste for music he retained to the end—indeed, when he was not murdering, music and flowers had always their appeal for him. He even went on to take 'minor orders' as a sub-deacon, so that his general conduct must certainly have been regarded as exemplary by the authorities of the church he attended. At this time he was in fact, as the presiding magistrate at his trial remarked, *un peu de l'église,* the suggestion being that it was to this early association with the Church that he owed the peculiar suavity of his manner, the ingratiating, confidence-creating way he undoubtedly had. But one is inclined to suspect that presiding magistrate of being something of an 'anti-clerical' in French politics, and of meaning to hint that it was from the Church Landru had learned how to impose upon credulous and foolish women. Rather one may suspect it was that smooth tongue of his which had enabled him to impose upon his ecclesiastical superiors and to hide from them his real disposition.

In various offices where he worked as a boy his conduct was still satisfactory, and when in due time he was called up for military service his army record remains good. He left at the expiration of his time with non-commissioned rank, and only then does he seem to have drifted in some way or another into the ranks of petty crime. Motors attracted him. He had again a certain skill as a mechanic— he claimed credit for one or two small inventions—and some offence connected with the buying or selling of a motor lorry earned him a sentence of three years. Soon after his release the police were looking for him again, but he managed to evade their attentions successfully. During his three years in prison his mother had died, and some time or another he had married. Apparently he was a good and kind husband, and no woman with whom he came in contact had ever a word of complaint to make against him—till at least in a moment of incredulous amazement they understood too late, and probably too briefly to understand in full; for surely one so efficient and painstaking as Landru, however he gave death, must have given it easily and swiftly.

To the credit of the French police, once they were convinced that Landru's wife had never had the least suspicion of the nature of his peculiar activities, they took care that neither she nor her children should be referred to. In the long trial once only something is said of "a good and simple woman who knew nothing of these things", and Landru himself does not omit to point out that he is admitted to have been a good husband and father. The French newspapers, too, either because they are so much less enterprising than our own or because they have more respect for the decencies of private life, make no reference to her. It is true that, owing to his unfortunate misunderstandings with the police, Landru was unable to live at home with his family, but he seems always to have kept in touch with them; and when, after one of his successful business transactions, he had to take over possession of furniture recently belonging to a woman now understood to be happily travelling in England or resident in Nice or somewhere else where furniture in a Paris apartment was no longer of value to her, then it was his son, a lad of sixteen or seventeen, whom he called upon to help convey it to the garage, where in due time so many oddities were to be poked out by interfering police officers.

There is an odd little scene recorded when at the Gambais villa this lad is seen in the garden picking flowers he explains he means to give to his mother; and Landru looks on approvingly, remarking that one cannot take too many pains to show attention to one's mother. He failed, however, to explain to the woman who was with him at the time—the one woman who visited Gambais and lived to tell the tale—that this mother was in fact his own wife and the boy his eldest son. But one cannot go into every detail, and the boy himself seems to have preserved an equally discreet silence, never forgetting the character of 'apprentice' assigned to him.

It is odd to notice, though, how all through this strange, dark tale of murder, ruthless and repeated and so callously efficient, there runs perpetually this motive of flowers and of music.

About Landru's personal appearance there does not seem to have been much to account for that success he had with the women whose complete confidence he won time and again. He is described as small, slight, insignificant; probably he owed his easy triumphs to his caressing, insinuating manner and his persuasive tongue, the tongue of the readiest liar, one imagines, that hell ever spawned.

Photographs show him as the almost comically typical representative of what the French call the *petit bourgeois*. It may be that the very ordinariness of his appearance helped to create that confidence he seems to have won so easily. Who could imagine that a man who looked so exactly like everyone else could be in fact so strangely, so dreadfully different? An old man could not have won such personal success, a young man might have been regarded with more suspicion, but why mistrust this plain, sober, tranquil, gentle-spoken man of middle age, whose middle-class respectability proclaimed itself aloud to all the world, who differed from the thousand like him only in being so much more polite, so extremely punctilious and well bred. Nor is there any Frenchwoman, whatever her station, but attaches importance to politeness and good breeding. No wonder Landru attracts, when in him good breeding is so ingrained that presently, on a bleak February dawn, when he has business in a Versailles square with, as the bitter Parisian jest ran at the time, the only 'widow' he has not known how to cheat, he refuses to recognize one of the officials whose duty it is to see that business well and truly carried out, until proper introductions have been effected!

Let the reader put the question to himself. Could he find it credible that the next typical clerk or shopman he sees hurrying to or from the city in the rush hours, bowler hat, umbrella, attaché case, season ticket, morning or evening paper under one arm, could he believe that man was a murderer not once but a dozen times, a murderer, too, so skilful and efficient that, grimmest of magicians, he could make the body of his victim vanish 'without trace'?

Always it is a part of the peculiar horror of this tale that makes it outstanding in the record of human wickedness, that everything is so drab, so ordinary, so commonplace, so 'everydayish' to quote the French expression. The actors in it are all the least conspicuous of folk, types of the everyday citizen whose ordinary destiny would be to slip unnoticed from undistinguished cradle by an uneventful and laborious life to one more grave in a crowded city cemetery—the Mr. and Mrs. Zero of our civilization, the tiniest of cogs in the revolving wheels that make society go round. All through the tale runs this 'dailiness of daily

life' till at the end, abruptly and without warning, leaps
up mystery and horror unparalleled.

When the amazing record of his crimes became known,
people began to talk of the hypnotic power of Landru's
eyes. They seem to have been small and bright under bushy
eyebrows, and he had a way of gazing into the distance as
though his immediate surroundings were unworthy of his
attention. Whether this was unconscious or a deliberate
pose on his part remains doubtful, but it was certainly
effective in impressing all who came in contact with him
with a certain quality in him of a proud and aloof tranquillity—and a proud and aloof tranquillity is not exactly
what one expects in a man accused of nearly a dozen murders. The murderer ferocious, the murderer brutal, greedy,
frenzied, passionate, we can understand, but not the murderer tranquil and gentle, the murderer who seems as if
he might turn from the corpse of his victim to give the cat
a saucer of milk or to chat over the fence with a neighbour
about the garden flowers.

Talk about hypnotic power may, however, be dismissed
as a discovery after the event. Possibly, too, the sketches
made in court give a better idea of Landru's personality
than the exact and precise photographs that misrepresent
the more because they misrepresent nothing. In the
sketches one seems to get a glimpse of a certain demoniac
power the man's deeds show that he possessed, however
well he kept it hidden in common life. There is one drawing, too, that shows him bending forward a little, his eloquent hands held out, his attitude full of an eager
sincerity, truth almost visibly oozing from him as he stands
there in the Versailles court-room before his judges, and
lies and lies and lies again with such conviction he almost
turns the false into the true.

The sketches, too, seem to show that the facial angle is

bad; though the presence of a heavy, close-growing beard makes the point a little difficult to decide with certainty. But the backward slope of the head is clearly marked, and is suggestive. Clearly marked, too, is the breadth of the head above the ear—an indication of the intellectual powers the man certainly possessed, in spite of the efforts of a famous English journalist to write him down a fool. A fool he certainly was not, except in that sense in which all sin is the supreme folly.

To give an instance of the clear insight that was at times in the man, however clouded by vanity and greed, it may be pointed out that the reason he gave for offering better prices for the furniture he was bargaining to acquire (thus by so unexpected a liberality earning the confidence of the gratified seller) was that after the war there was likely to be a great scarcity of manufactured goods, so that anyone with a store laid up would be able to sell at a big profit.

The reflection seems obvious to-day, commonplace indeed. To have entertained it, however, at that time—while the war still raged—is proof of exceptional insight. Some of those to whom that same insight came were led by it to fortune. One remembers, for instance, how the British Government offered for sale by public contract some enormous collection or another of textiles manufactured for war use, and how there was at first considerable hesitation to buy. When at last one speculator plucked up courage and ventured the purchase, he was able to sell again retail at a profit that made him a millionaire in a month or two.

So might it easily have been with Landru, since he was of those who had acumen enough to realize the famine of the world for those commodities of which the war had so long deprived it. Had Landru but followed the gleam thus vouchsafed him he might well, with his talent for buying and selling and his passion for method and precision, have

acquired prosperity and wealth and all the honour and re-
nown that wealth brings with it. Instead he chose another
path, possibly arguing that since public slaughter had become the business of all the world, a little private slaughter
might be permitted to the individual.

A very noticeable feature of his physical make-up was
his baldness. It seems to have struck the imagination of
the Parisian public, perhaps because there is something
respectable, almost avuncular about baldness; one finds it
difficult to imagine a bald Don Juan, to conceive a bald
Lothario making a conquest of two hundred and eighty-
three women—for that is the incredible and altogether pre-
posterous number of the women that the careful investigation of the Paris police established as the count of his
fiancées. Though one may be permitted to doubt whether
in all those cases actual *fiançailles* had been announced,
for in France the *fiançailles* is a serious and public affair.
But still, in this incredible business one may believe anything—even two hundred and eighty-three fiancées. Perhaps, like Clive, Landru stood amazed at his own
moderation when he reflected that out of them all he had
contented himself with murdering only ten—at least that
is all the prosecution brought forward, with one boy
thrown in as if for makeweight.

If, however, Landru had lost his hair Nature had com-
pensated him with the gift of a magnificent and luxurious
beard. To-day beards are out of fashion; but in France, at
that time, they still had their admirers, and Landru's appears to have played its part in the success of its owner's
numerous courtships. Maybe it was gratitude for this as-
sistance that made him show concern for it at the last and
emulate Sir Thomas More in expressing a solicitude for
its safety from the touch of steel. No doubt a beard may
be regarded as a symbol of respectability, and we can no

more imagine Don Juan bearded than bald. All that there is of middle-age responsibility, of middle-class respectability, may be looked on as embodied in the beard; the beard that, so to speak, waved Landru on through his two hundred and eighty-three successive conquests.

In every description of him there are two points that continually emerge, that are always commented on. The first is the unstudied composure of the man, the quiet and slightly distant courtesy in which he never failed. There was about him a kind of haughty indifference that seemed to lift him above the fret and fuss of everyday experience, even when that everyday experience was trial for his life. The second detail that is commonly remarked upon is the long slenderness of his nervous fingers, eloquent and caressing—and something more as well. Easy to picture them caressing with tender gentleness an infatuated woman, stroking a tired forehead, stroking more softly still the worn cheeks, stealing down as gentle as silk to twine themselves about the throat till all at once they tighten, all in an instant turning into so fierce, so murderous, so effective a grip, the victim would scarcely have time to recognize the change from the pretence of love to the reality of death.

Of Landru, in his domestic capacity, we have perhaps the most intimate picture ever presented of the murderer at home. Charles Peace, too, seems to have had a pleasant domestic side to his character and a taste for music as marked as Landru's—there seems no record that Peace shared Landru's passion for flowers—but no such picture of Peace in his fireside slippers is extant as that provided of Landru in a little pamphlet sold at the time on the streets of Paris and written by a Mlle Fernande Segret, she who enjoys the unique experience of being the only woman who visited the Gambais villa in Landru's company and came away again alive.

"Voilà mon petit Paradis," said he the first time he took her there, though one may justifiably complain that *petit Paradis* is hardly a well-chosen term for this private slaughter-house, this secluded shambles whereto, as to the lion's den in the story, so many footsteps led but none returned.

One wonders why he spared her. It cannot have been because she had no money. One of his assassinations brought him no more than two francs, which seems poor pay for what must really be a troublesome and tedious job—even for an expert—hardly enough, indeed, to cover the 'overhead'. Was he really fond of her? It hardly seems likely that he could be fond of anyone, but then with Landru anything is possible. He may merely have felt that there was no hurry, or more likely she owned her safety to the fact that she was in more intimate relations with her family, and a disappearance too abrupt might have set them worrying for details of her fate. Most of his other victims, it will be remembered, were solitary folk, with few friends or relatives and none likely to make prompt inquiry.

At the trial Mlle Segret described herself as *artiste lyrique,* though she omitted to supply details of her professional engagements and qualifications. At the time she met Landru she was working as an assistant in a shop, and she gives a long description of the classic 'pick up', how in a tram one day she and a companion observed a fellow-passenger—male—looking at them; how when they alighted he alighted too; how he spoke to them and was duly and properly snubbed; how nevertheless he persisted, warning them gravely of the dangers young women encountered who went alone about the streets of Paris; how gradually his persistence and more especially his courtesy and air of breeding—*un vrai monsieur* always, it will be noticed—impressed her, till finally he is permitted to call at her home.

There, too, the impression he makes is favourable. It always was. He proposed marriage—by this time, with his score approaching the fourth hundred, he must have been acquiring a certain facility in this—he is accepted and he proves himself the ideal lover. His betrothed grows almost lyrical, *artiste lyrique* in fact, as she describes his courteous attentions—the *petit soins*—his kindness and his thoughtfulness, the presents he makes her. A veritable bower of flowers she describes his room, on one occasion when she and her mother—for the proprieties must be observed—go there to dine with him. And then his intellectual tastes! Among novelists his favourite author was Balzac; his favourite bedside book *Le Disciple*, by Paul Bourget. How many happy hours they spent together, reading these and other classics of French literature! In poetry his taste was equally refined, and he would often recite with admirable effect the verses of de Musset, Lamartine, and others of similar standing. In music he certainly preferred the lighter, gayer tunes to more severe compositions, but he had merely contempt for the music-hall; childish, he found it, and void of intellectual interest.

Altogether an admirable picture, and this idyllic courtship took its pleasant intellectual course with only two drawbacks; one, Landru's habit of vanishing now and again, presumably when it was time for another murder to be committed, wherefrom he would return to his flowers, his books and music, his pleasantly intellectual intercourse with his betrothed, all the grave and sober routine of his well-regulated life.

Once he rebuked a certain too great liking for the theatre he seems to have detected in Mlle Segret, with the remark that one could well give up visiting the theatre when life itself presented to the onlooker so rich a feast of comedy. It was at any rate a comedy that he was doing his best to turn into a tragedy.

The second drawback was that the promised marriage seemed a long time in getting itself celebrated. Not that Landru, to whom plausible excuse was as natural as breathing, lacked good and plentiful explanations. In his usual character of refugee from the invaded districts he had no papers, and in France there is little one can do, and nothing official, without papers. But official arrangements had been made to meet the case of those refugees who had lost these necessary documents, and finally Mlle Segret and her mother (who appears to have had her suspicions) went to visit the mayor of the particular town in which, for them, Landru had situated that prosperous factory of his prewar days. Alas! the mayor had never heard either of Landru or his factory. But Landru, though a little hurt at this display of a certain lack of confidence, had his explanation ready. The mayor, an old friend, had been so worried by innumerable inquiries that finally he had adopted the expedient of denying everybody and everything!

As explanation, it cannot be counted among Landru's happiest efforts. Still, it served its purpose, and presently (the question of marriage slipping into the background) Mlle Segret is seen established as Landru's 'companion' as she discreetly expresses it. As pseudo-husband he proved as kind, thoughtful, attentive, as he had been as suitor, and proudly she records that when she went with him to visit friends she would receive many congratulations on her alliance with a man so gay, so charming, always the life and soul of the party, so evidently superior in intellect and breeding.

Once or twice again he took her to the Gambais villa and still, unlike all his other feminine companions, she had the luck to return alive. The way in which the villagers stared at him and her worried her a little, but he explained carelessly that country people were always like that, they always stared at every visitor from Paris—and then he would resume humming his favourite tune: *Adieu, notre petite table.* Mlle Segret does not seem to have cared much for the Gambais villa. She found it of a "comfort only relative." In her character of good housewife she discovered that the bedding was apt to grow damp during their absences. But she seems never to have noticed anything suspicious, and such cooking as was necessary she carried out on the kitchen stove with no thought that it had ever been put to uses quite other than domestic.

She was always willing enough to return to their cosy Paris flat, where life passed so pleasantly, and the only drawback those mysterious absences that Landru still indulged in and from which he would return more smiling, more amiable, more courteous than ever—and also plentifully supplied with money; often, for example, with a government bond or two for sale, recently transferred to him by the elderly widow or spinster to whom it had originally belonged and concerning whose present whereabouts her former neighbours were idly wondering.

But presently the secret of these absences was explained; presumably Mlle Segret's curiosity was becoming so strong that something had to be done to satisfy it. So one day Landru confessed to her that he was in police employ, there were at times errands of special importance which he had to undertake at the request of the police authorities. He made the confession—the word is used advisedly—with considerable reluctance, for in France the 'flic' enjoys no such respect and confidence as we in En-

gland accord to those who defend society against its law-
less enemies. He would give it up as soon as he possibly
could, he promised, and indeed of promises his stock was
always inexhaustible; and meanwhile here was the explanation of his sudden and mysterious absences.

In the intervals of these absences he was busy with all
sorts and kinds of projects. But here Mlle Segret inter-
poses an acute psychological observation. Never, she says,
did she see him work with perseverance; never could he
keep his mind fixed for long on any one project. For a
hall-mark of the criminal mind is this incapacity for steady
application. Steady and regular employ is abhorrent to it,
the result of an inherent weakness of the will unable to
remain for long faithful to one idea. Again and again in
criminological studies one comes across this weakness of
willpower that Landru's 'companion' notes when she records his failure to keep constant to any one of his numerous designs.

None the less his affairs seemed prosperous enough,
and one day in the Rue de Rivoli they observed and jointly
admired a dinner service, richly gilt and of an exquisite
pattern. It was a fine sunny spring morning, they were
both in happy mood; Landru because his affairs were going so well, Mlle Segret because a day or two before he
had promised her a speedy wedding.

Was it a promise that he meant to perform? Legally, it
was impossible, since he had already wife and family. One
wonders if perhaps that offer was but the first step towards
another trip to Gambais, for which this time of the two
railway tickets purchased one would have been a single
only!

Impossible to say, for as it happened a relative of one
of the women who had made one of those trips to Gambais, for which one ticket had needed to be a single only,

was also enjoying a stroll in the sunshine that fine April
morning. While Landru and his companion were consult-
ing over the purchase of that dinner service which would
be such an addition to their home, this relative of the vanished woman was in his turn watching them. When they
made up their minds to effect the purchase and entered the
shop, he entered close behind. He heard the bargaining,
he heard Landru explaining that he had not enough money
in his pocket to pay on the spot the full amount required.
But he would pay a hundred francs on account and the rest
on delivery. The shopkeeper was more than willing. And
monsieur's address? Landru gave it, the shopkeeper noted
it down, repeating it aloud to make sure he had it correct.
Landru confirmed it as correct, and pleased and excited
as children with their new purchase he and Mlle Segret
went off home to be ready to receive it, while that other
customer, whom they had hardly noticed, hurried round
to the police to tell them he had found at last the mysterious individual in whose company his aunt had last been
seen before her sudden, complete, and inexplicable disappearance.

Early next morning, about seven—Landru, industrious
man, had already been out, probably to his garage, and
had just returned for the continental breakfast of coffee
and a roll—two veritable *agents de la Sûreté* knocked at
his door. When he understood their errand, though surely
he must have known this was the end, must have felt the
chill of death strike into his soul, he showed only his presently familiar attitude of a proud and tranquil indifference.
"What! Arrest me in my own home!" he exclaimed, scandalized at this departure from his own high standard of
breeding and correctitude. But that indeed was the purpose of his visitors and one they proceeded forthwith to

carry out. Mlle Segret expressed her natural dismay and earned a rebuke from Landru.

"Don't trouble your head about all this," he commanded. "It will be easily arranged."

But the arrangement was not to be so easy as all that, though the long battle that Landru was now to fight against all the forces of the law is as remarkable as any recorded in the legal history of any country.

As for Mlle Segret, she was destined to see him only twice more: once, that same evening, when, his first interrogation over, she was allowed to say him farewell, and ne with a touch of sentiment whispered to her the words of his favourite tune, *"Adieu! notre petite table";* and once more in the Versailles court when she appeared there to give some not very important evidence, and it was observed that he was as tranquilly indifferent to her as he was to all the long line of witnesses who bored him with their dull and interminable testimony.

III The Murderer as Captain of his Soul

It was in April 1919 when this arrest was carried out, and the relaxation of the pressure of the war—that war of which Landru had once scandalized the Segret family by remarking it was ending too soon for him—permitted the police to give the affair more attention than might have otherwise been possible.

There had been, it was noticed at the time, a touch of quite incredulous horror in the voice of that first examining magistrate when he told Landru he was accused of no less than "four assassinations!" The tale was not to stop there. Poking about in the garage Landru used as a kind of warehouse, the police found the oddest things. A bunch of false hair, for example, presently identified as having belonged to Mme Buisson. Now where was Mme Buisson for whom indeed her family had been searching for some time? And then the papers of identity of that young girl, Andrée Babelay, who in the morning of her life had come in contact with Landru, is for a moment seen laughing and chatting with him and calling him by his pet name, and then is no more heard of. If she was still in life, why had she parted with these papers without which indeed no French citizen is officially alive at all? How, for instance, without them could she have obtained the new situation Landru explained she had left him to secure?

Inconceivably, grotesquely, incredibly, the number mounted, and further back into the past extended the police inquiries. Back through the long years of the war they traced Landru's peculiar activities, finally ending their researches just before its outbreak, in the summer of 1914, when Landru had smiled his way into the friendship and the confidence of a Madame Cuchet, a widow who possessed a son of eighteen and certain property. They lived together, widow, son, and Landru, at the Vernouillet villa; and there, after a time, Landru continued to live alone. Madame and her son, he explained, had gone to England for reasons that might be guessed, since at that time many widows with only sons were torn between the claims of patriotism and those of maternal affection but that he, Landru, would never betray, since whatever the reason was it had been given to him in confidence.

The investigation continued, and gradually Paris and the world began to hear rumours of this incredible reincarnation of the Bluebeard of the nursery tales. When it became known that Landru had made conquest of nearly three hundred feminine hearts, Paris fairly gasped, and could not even resist a certain feeling of bewildered admiration. A man with close on three hundred fiancées—

'formidable'. The thing seemed to pass into the fantastic, the unreal, it took on the quality of some fairy-tale of the heroic age when everything was on a larger scale than in cramped modern days! The horror and tragedy and the mystery of the fate of all these unlucky women grew half forgotten, while Landru's bald head shone through a score of music-hall sketches, his beard wagged on every cabaret stage, the two hundred and eighty-three fiancées became the staple fare of every jester and comedian avid of easy applause, till there was hardly a theatre audience but was ready to rock with laughter at the mere mention of the number—two hundred and eighty and three! It seemed as if to so incredible a horror laughter had become the only possible reaction.

Then, too, it began to be known that the police were not finding Landru an easy person to deal with. Confronted with a mass of overwhelming evidence, he admitted nothing, he had an explanation for all—or else the noblest, most chivalrous of motives for offering none. One had to be careful, too; all the niceties had to be observed. If his spectacles were mislaid, for instance, the whole investigation had to be suspended till they were found again. Any new magistrate or police officer coming into the affair had to be duly presented to Landru and their credentials shown or he would have nothing to do with them. Never, in fact, was there such a stickler for etiquette, never a man more ready to stand upon every formality—and never once did he weaken, hesitate, alter in any way his attitude of imperturbable and tranquil indifference, as of one for whom all these things had but a passing and temporary interest.

And let it be remembered that in France such investigations are not carried out with any such scrupulous consideration for the convenience and the rights and the susceptibilities of the suspected person as must be shown in England. In France the sole object is to get at the truth, and to that aim all else is subordinated. In England also the object is to get at the truth, but often, as it seems, on condition that nothing must be said or done to hurt the feelings of the accused. In France there are no judge's rules that the police are expected to be governed by under penalty of being held up to universal execration for the practice of brutal and unfair methods. No French police officer giving evidence risks being asked in horror-stricken tones by defending counsel: "Were you not endeavouring to induce the prisoner to confess?" And if a confession is produced in France it is assumed to be true, in England the assumption appears to be that it must be proof of innocence, since no one would confess except under the pressure of a brutal and unscrupulous police, to which again only the innocent could succumb!

From April 1919 till November 1921 the investigation continued, while Paris giggled over the incredible tale, and Landru, imperturbable and tranquil as ever, submitted to innumerable confrontations, questionings, reconstructions, without for one moment weakening or faltering or varying his perpetual response: "You bring these accusations against me? Well, it is your business to prove them. Do so."

It was a task that was not showing itself so easy. Ample, overwhelming evidence there was that all these women had last been seen in Landru's company and then never seen again. But there the proof ended abruptly. Landru's simple explanation was that they had gone about their own affairs. He had had certain purely business transactions with them, conducted no doubt in a pleasant, social manner. Even in business one had to respect the courtesies. But, the business concluded, they had parted with mutual esteem, and he knew nothing of what had happened to them afterwards. Why should he? Was every business man to be responsible for the future of every client he dealt with?

So it went on all through the two and a half long years of the investigation, and not all the efforts of the most skilled, the most experienced police officers in Paris could draw from Landru any single admission. They took him to the villa at Vernouillet, to the Gambais villa he had once so inappropriately described as his *'petit Paradis'*; they showed him carcasses of sheep being consumed in that stove in the kitchen he had been careful, they reminded him, to have installed when he first rented the villa, and he still looked on with his air of mild and tranquil interest. They pointed out that his consumption of fuel had been large, and he explained that those dishonest neighbours of his had taken advantage of his absences in Paris to raid his store of coal. Only once did he make an admission that seems a little enlightening. One of his victims had had two pet dogs, and there was proof that, after she had vanished from the Villa Tric, her two dogs were still there. How had he disposed of them, then? It was a point that might be of interest. At last he explained. He had strangled them.

"It is the gentlest and easiest of deaths," he added, and only in the silence that followed, only when he saw how those to whom he had spoken were looking at him did he appear to realize that in that sentence might be found a significance of its own.

Finally, he was brought before a jury in a little courtroom at Versailles, and *'tout Paris'* flocked to hear the trial of this man who had become something of a legend. Every woman with a new hat or frock to show took it to Versailles to display; no actress with a flair for publicity could afford to be seen elsewhere while the court was sitting; no man of the world but quickly lost his reputation if he could not recount the latest Landru story.

For Landru did not disappoint. To the end he preserved his ready tongue, his quick wit, his impressive air of tranquil disdain for all this fuss; his open, and not unrighteous, contempt, for the horde of gaping, scrambling spectators; his dignified assumption of complete innocence; above all, his attitude that if the prosecution alleged these things against him then it was their business to produce proof of what they said. Negligently he would drop hints from time to time that his innocence would be established, the prosecution for ever confounded, when two or three of his pretended victims would appear in court alive and well as was altogether likely to happen, Landru promised, in a day or two, though indeed, in fact, it has not happened yet.

There appeared in the witness box a long line of witnesses and each day the court was littered with the strangest collection of bits of furniture, old clothing, cheap furs, and so on and so on, melancholy relics that drew from one witness a cry of real emotion.

"If my sister were alive," she exclaimed, "never would she have parted with these things of hers she was always so proud of and always took such care of."

It was perhaps the nearest the prosecution ever got to establishing that main fact they had to establish, and whereof they never succeeded in producing strict legal proof—evidence, that is, of the actual death of any single one of all those whose names figured on the long *acte d'accusation*. Evidence in plenty that each one had last been seen in Landru's company, evidence as much as could be wished that afterwards no friend or relative had had any further news, that promises to write had not been ful-

filled, that their possessions, their property, their most intimate belongings had passed into Landru's hands, but of
how, if he had murdered, those murders had been carried
out, of how afterwards the bodies had been disposed of;
on those points the prosecution had frankly to avow there
was nothing to be said with certainty.

In the courtyard of the Gambais villa, it is true, a few
handfuls of charred bones and a collection of human teeth
had been found. But then close by was the Gambais cemetery with an ossuary full of human bones that all the
children of the village had access to. And it was proved,
too, that the key of the villa had for some time been in
the care of a man of deficient intelligence. Who could tell
what tricks might have been played by that disordered intelligence, by the malice or mistaken zeal of neighbours,
by the mischief of children, or even by the police themselves? How tempting to throw down a few burnt bones
to provide the evidence admittedly lacking!

True, again, there were various witnesses to depose that
thick fumes of smoke and even gleams of fire, had been
seen coming from the chimney of the Villa Tric, busy as
any factory. The gleams of fire had been seen, according
to the evidence, on a dark night. Easy enough at once to
turn up the records and prove that particular night was
particularly clear. Another witness spoke of a smell of
burnt flesh, and the court was visibly affected till Landru
woke from his usual haughty and tranquil indifference.
Ah, yes, he remembered. It was one day when some cut-
lets were being cooked for dinner and by inexcusable neglect they had been burnt to a cinder. No doubt—with a
courteous inclination of the head towards the witness—that
was the occasion to which madame referred.

Then again, one police officer bicycling very early in
the morning in the district on some errand connected with

the case, had observed with interest that long line of lorries which every morning brought thousands of tons of refuse from Paris to dump in old quarries and disused gravel pits in the Rambouillet forest. He had imagined that Landru, too, that busy and observant man, might one morning have watched this daily procession. Not difficult perhaps if one had burnt a body in a stove to heap together the remains, the unconsumed portions, the ashes in general, in a convenient parcel and deposit them at night, where in the morning they would be buried for ever under fresh tons of Paris refuse from all the dustbins of the multitudinous city.

He had put the theory before his superiors and they had listened and been interested. But where was your proof? If that had been Landru's method, no one had seen him about his black business in the black night, nor could it be hoped that after months and even years of the deposit of so many tons of refuse, the secret they hid, if indeed they hid it, could be discovered.

Landru had been also, it was proved, a frequent purchaser of saws, and saws may be used for other things than those small carpentering jobs and alterations he had undoubtedly carried out. But then again what proof is there in that? At the end all that could be shown as possible relics of ten women and a boy was just a few scraps of burnt bones and a collection of human teeth. For the rest, nothing but idle conjecture and the aloof and patient smile of Landru.

Yet the imagination boggles a little at this picture of the man carrying out his murders, dissecting and burning to ashes the body with such neat dexterity, disposing of those ashes with equal efficiency, and then returning to Paris, courteous, smiling, pleasant as ever, probably humming his favourite tune, *Adieu, notre petite table,* and resuming there his sober, respectable, well-ordered life with its flowers, its music, its poetic recitations and literary discussions.

Nor was the prosecution more successful in establishing the method. There was no trace or spot of blood to be found anywhere, no sign of any struggle. Poison? Yes, there was a book treating of poison in his possession, but nothing to show that Landru had ever purchased anything of the sort. One remembers, though, those long and slender fingers of his, and that remark he once dropped that strangling is the gentlest of deaths. It is also, as every doctor knows, a method of inflicting death in which an extraordinary degree of perfection can be attained.

So the long duel went on, with Landru never at a loss and seldom disappointing an audience that had come to expect his epigrams, and was indeed ready, such was not his reputation, to laugh at them before they were well uttered, just as to-day Mr. Bernard Shaw has only to rise from his place to have his audience already on the giggle. Not that Landru always encouraged laughter. Temperamental as any other spoilt favourite of the public, sometimes he would turn on his audience and rend it with contempt and scorn.

"There is nothing to laugh at, I defend my life," he flashed out once when there was too much laughter in court.

Some of his replies, too, are undeniably effective.

"How could I foresee," he demands, when urged to explain some of the entries in that curious note-book of his, "that one day I should be asked to remember such trifling details?"

"My accounts were not kept with a view of satisfying a police inquiry," he protests on another occasion; and when pressed to say why he had not offered to the examining magistrate a specially ingenious explanation he had just produced, he had his reply ready: "Oh, he and I, we were not on very good terms," he explains.

Occasionally, too, he does not hesitate to rebuke his judges when they fall short of his own high standard of breeding. The presiding judge had chanced to mention that one of the vanished women had given her age as 39, though in reality it was 44. Landru is shocked.

"Ah, monsieur le juge," he says, "I should never have told that."

Now and then his patience wears a little thin.

"Every time you find a figure in my note-book, you call it an assassination," he cries, and when told that his explanations are not simple, he answered: "You mean you do not take them simply."

Always he keeps in his replies to that high standard of courtesy, that innate breeding, which had so struck all these women who unfortunately were not in court to bear testimony to its charm. Again and again he is pressed to explain why, as his note-book entries show, when he took them to Gambais he bought always one single ticket and one return.

"I could hardly buy a return ticket for a lady," he answers at last with a deprecatory movement of the hand.

Obviously a man of breeding could not suggest to a lady that her sojourn was to be limited by anything but her own will.

And his possession of the most personal, private effects he explains in the same way:

"Madame did not wish that things like that should be seen by third persons," he explains with a delicate hint of rebuke to these coarse-minded lawyers and police who had been pulling them about and peering at them and examining them with little thought of the rules of good breeding.

"Ah, Monsieur le Président, we seek the truth together," he assures that gentleman on one occasion; and later he rebukes him gently: "Do not let us try to find a tragedy everywhere," he urges; and another time he says loftily that his private life concerns neither the public nor the law.

So it continues all through the three long weeks of his trial, while the world waited for the verdict and all Paris fought for a seat at what had become something like a public entertainment. Once indeed the crush became so great that Landru was moved to offer his own place to anyone who cared to occupy it. On an outburst of temper occurring between some of the lawyers in the case, one of those professional disputes that are almost a matter of etiquette and custom, and on one of them threatening to retire, Landru is openly sympathetic.

"I also I could wish to retire from the case," he observes.

All through these lighter interludes, however, he clung to his main point. He was not there to prove anything. The prosecution accused him of certain things, and it was their business to prove what they advanced. For himself, he knew nothing about the ladies mentioned, who had presumably gone about their business. On certain points his tongue was sealed—to him private life was sacred. On other points he could say nothing for he did not remember the exact details, and he would suggest nothing that he could not prove. Once indeed his feelings overcame him, and he exclaimed:

"I am deeply hurt that I am not believed."

His composure never leaves him. All through the long ordeal of the three weeks' trial he shows himself as much the master of himself, the captain of his soul, as in the still longer, still more trying ordeal of those thirty months when day by day he was being questioned, and day by day being faced with new facts, new details, new demands for fresh explanations, days when he had to fight alone against all the resources of trained, expert, experienced officers of police.

Whence then did this man draw his unconquerable firmness? The inspiration of the hero and the martyr one can understand, but this strangler of women, this multiple assassin, this huckster of stolen furniture, this unimaginable liar, whence his? Is it that the Creator has stamped the human soul so greatly with His own impress that never is it wholly lost? How poor and thin before such a spectacle do those theories seem that would proclaim man the creature of his endocrine glands. Is it then the secretions of the glands that can make of the same man a strangler of helpless, solitary women and gift him with a soul of rocklike fortitude?

But the end had come now, and on November 30, 1921, the jury returned a verdict of guilty, adding, somewhat surprisingly, a recommendation to mercy that, equally surprisingly, the relatives of the murdered women sign as well. In fact, everyone seems to have signed except Landru himself, who refused with his usual aloof and cold indifference.

Epilogue

But before there is enacted the final scene, Landru had one more card to play, and apparently he played it for pure love of the game since he must have known by now there was no trick left that it could take.

A few hours before his execution, when it was perfectly

certain there would be no reprieve, he asked for paper and pen and composed a long letter to Monsieur Godefroy, the, as we should say, leading counsel for the prosecution. It is nearly two thousand words in length, say a newspaper column and a half. The handwriting is clear, neat and regular, there are few corrections, there is no sign of mental agitation, it is written with a facility that would do credit to a practised journalist and a sense of drama a novelist might be proud of.

The purport is to describe the trial in terms of a long duel between a consciously innocent Landru and a prosecuting counsel in whose mind Landru depicts a constant struggle between an original conviction of the prisoner's guilt and a tumult of growing doubt. He draws a contrast between his powerful adversary, the trained experienced lawyer with all the resources of the State behind him, and the writer of the letter, solitary, alone, a prisoner, kept in ignorance of all. With extraordinary skill Landru paints the surprise, the doubt, the hesitation he persists he saw invading the lawyer's mind, the effort to expel them, their return again and again, stronger than ever, while all the time Landru himself, superior and pitying, follows with a detached interest the course of this inner battle. In spite of the indifference and detachment Landru had assumed in court, he must have watched the opposing lawyers with the closest attention, for he can reproduce their gestures, remember their expressions, and always put on each his own interpretation of an increasing and troubled sense of his innocence that they, on their side, were trying to suppress. He reminds M. Godefroy of little discrepancies in the evidence and pretends to have noted how they brought him an increasing disquiet. Towards the end of the letter he draws a poetic picture of that *petit Paradis* at Gambais he knows M. Godefroy has visited, and asks him, with a passing reference to Werther, if a place so lovely could possibly have been the scene of such crimes as the prosecution have imagined? The lawyer is supposed to have felt this, and impatient with himself and his growing doubts, to have decided to end it, crying loudly but in ill-assured tones: "No pity, strike without fear."

The letter is as incredible a production as is everything else connected with this case. Remember that the thing was written by a man undoubtedly guilty of eleven sordid and brutal murders, and now on the very eve of paying the last penalty. It concludes with the assurance that the writer would die innocent and tranquil, and he hopes, but evidently with little confidence, that M. Godefroy may be able to say the same when his time comes.

A few hours after the completion of this extraordinary epistle the writer is dead, and of his execution there is one detail that may be noted. So thin, so worn, so frail had he become that when he was thrown on the plank of the guillotine his weight was too small to set in action automatically the knife, as should have been the case. The executioner had himself to release it before it would fall.

There is proof there that though his mind had remained firm and calm and tranquil to the end, his body had felt the strain. But he retained his courtesy and his sense of breeding to the end. Almost his last words were an apology to the priest on duty for not attending mass because, he said, speaking of his guards and executioners, he would be sorry "to keep these gentlemen waiting".